NOV - - 2016

SHIELD
OF
STRAW

 VERTICAL.

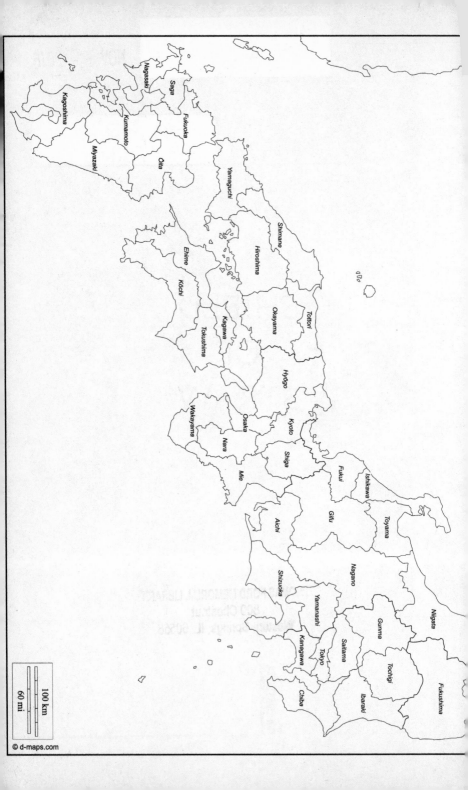

SHIELD
OF
STRAW

Kazuhiro Kiuchi

Translated by Asumi Shibata

 VERTICAL.

Published by Vertical, Inc., New York, 2016

Originally published in Japanese as *Wara no Tate* in 2004
and reissued in paperback in 2007.

ISBN 978-1-941220-55-9

Manufactured in the United States of America

First Edition

Vertical, Inc.
451 Park Avenue South, 7th Floor
New York, NY 10016
www.vertical-inc.com

TABLE OF CONTENTS

To my late father—

SHIELD
OF
STRAW

In the eyes of God, no matter how much humans struggle to prolong our lives, we're merely charging out onto the battlefield with a shield of straw.

—Richard Hancock

Prologue

"From the Metropolitan Police Department to all precincts, we've been informed of a prone body in Kitazawa jurisdiction. It's close to the fifth block of South Matsubara. A nearby precinct, please report, over."

"Kitazawa 5, Umeoka third block."

"Metropolitan Police Department, roger. Kitazawa 5, head to the scene. Location is a copse in the fifth block of South Matsubara. The report was filed by a man called Mamiya who was walking his dog. He spotted a person lying face down on the ground. The lower body was exposed. Most likely a child. Most likely female. No confirmation as to whether she is dead or alive. Over."

"Kitazawa 5, roger that."

"To Kitazawa, reference number 7701, call at 4:09, this is Sakai, assigned to this case, over."

"Kitazawa, roger. This is Ichinose, likewise on this case."

"MPD, roger. Over."

His granddaughter, Chika, hadn't returned yet.

Takaoki Ninagawa's heart was acting up. He'd been hospitalized twice before. He waited for the Isosorbide mononitrate pill to dissolve on his tongue.

Chika attended a private elementary school in Setagaya

Ward. She was to enter second grade next month. The school was just a twenty-minute walk from home even at a child's pace. She usually came back at around four o'clock. After arriving home, she'd head straight to Ninagawa's room.

Chika's mother Masumi had worried about Ninagawa's heart condition and offered him words of comfort while it had still been light out, but now that the sun had fallen over the horizon she was silent.

It was a kidnapping.

Ninagawa was sure of it.

Takaoki Ninagawa was one of Japan's most affluent men. He'd started at an insignificant amplifier manufacturing company and built up an enormous corporate group whose crown jewel was a world-renowned home electronics manufacturer. Affiliated companies numbered over one thousand two hundred. Ninagawa had passed the position of CEO on to his successor but remained the lead shareholder, and the group was his empire.

He'd already contacted Chika's school, according to whom she'd left at the same time as always. Ninagawa's family and retainers, along with people from the school, were now searching all over for Chika.

None of them had reported in yet.

"We can't let the police know."

Those had been Ninagawa's strict orders.

"The kidnapper wants money. Give him as much as he wants. If Chika is safe, I don't care."

Ninagawa waited with bated breath for the kidnapper to call. Yet even after midnight, the phone hadn't trilled.

What if Chika never returned?

Impossible, Ninagawa denied the idea with all his heart. Yet anxiety reared its head soon again.

The crippling fear threatened to destroy him.

Despite not feeling sleepy in the slightest, Ninagawa nearly blanked out all of a sudden. He was ashamed. How pathetic was he, almost falling asleep when he didn't know what kind of predicament, what fear and suffering, Chika might be facing?

The sun was about to rise when the phone finally rang.

Masumi leapt to the phone.

"What? The police?"

Masumi collapsed to the floor, still holding the receiver.

Ninagawa understood. Chika wasn't coming home.

He clutched his chest and sank to the floor. He was dimly aware of his consciousness receding.

Just let me die like this!

His cry went unvoiced.

Chika Ninagawa's remains were found in a copse within Setagaya Ward. An elderly man walking his dog shortly before dawn had called in the report.

Her lower body had been stripped, and she had been raped before being beaten to death.

The Metropolitan Police Department's Investigation Section One joined the Kitazawa Police Station to establish a special investigation headquarters. Witness reports and the crime's M.O. brought one suspect to the fore.

Kunihide Kiyomaru.

Arrested for murdering a girl using a similar method seven years ago, he'd been granted parole by Sendai Prison the previous year.

Investigators were immediately dispatched to confirm Kiyomaru's whereabouts, but he had already disappeared. The special investigation HQ ran a DNA test on the body fluids left on Chika's body and compared it with the data on Kiyomaru from the case seven years ago.

A perfect match—Kunihide Kiyomaru was wanted nationwide.

By the time Ninagawa came to, Chika's body had already been sent to the crematory.

Chika had died; why was Ninagawa still alive?

Outside the window of his suite at the university hospital where he'd been admitted, cherry blossoms were in full bloom.

Why was he still alive?

Out of consideration for Ninagawa, who was a prominent sponsor of the reigning Liberal Democratic Party, the National Police Agency had issued a stern order to prefectural police across the country to solve the case as soon as possible. Despite an unusually thorough dragnet, however, they had yet to sniff out any trace of Kiyomaru.

Even if he was arrested, what of it?

Ninagawa was well aware that even a horrible criminal who had stolen two young lives could not be put to death in the framework of Japan's extant legal system.

Ninagawa was seventy-six years old. He had a heart disease.

He wasn't exactly counting down the days to his death, but neither was he guaranteed years more.

He would find no peace in death if Kiyomaru continued to exist in this world after his own passing.

He made a decision.

Tasking a trusted subordinate, Ninagawa began to search for an individual who could grant his wish.

He mobilized all of his connections in the political sphere, the business world, and even underground to seek out the kind of talent he required. He didn't hold back on spending. He didn't state any specifics but conveyed that he was in need of someone who could handle a big job regardless of its legality.

Everyone who became aware of Ninagawa's actions couldn't help but think "revenge."

Yet the culprit, Kiyomaru, was still on the loose. Despite the police's extensive search net, no one knew where he was. What did Ninagawa think he could do?

No one could possibly grant his wish.

Almost ten days after Ninagawa began his search, a man contacted him. The fellow had somehow gotten wind of the request and come to offer his services.

Ninagawa felt inclined to meet this individual who'd come out of nowhere.

Having created a vast business empire from scratch, Ninagawa was confident that he had an eye for people. He wasn't fooled by titles or resumes. He had a nose for talent.

When the man entered Ninagawa's suite, the temperature in the room seemed to drop a few degrees.

The man simply identified himself as "Saraya." Ninagawa had never come across such a surname and had no idea what characters it used in writing.

A diminutive middle-aged man in a cheap business suit.

Yet his presence was overwhelming. Just being in the same room as him made it difficult to breathe.

A negative presence, so to speak.

When Ninagawa was little, he used to sense someone standing in the darkness behind him every time he went to the restroom in the middle of the night. Yet, unable to turn around, he would hastily finish his business and scamper down the hallway with his eyes closed until he could dive under his mother's futon. That feeling came back to him now.

This man could be either in his forties or past sixty. His expression could have been a faint smile or a brave front.

If the Devil really exists, Ninagawa thought, *perhaps his face would look like this.*

Ninagawa told him everything. He also floated a large monetary compensation.

Saraya listened without the slightest change in his expression. "I'll accept the job," he said.

However, he added.

"Only if you're serious about this…"

Of course Ninagawa was serious. This wasn't something you joked about.

"So you're sure? There's no going back."

Ninagawa didn't care. He was already at the point of no

return.

He couldn't leave this life with regrets even if it meant never reaching heaven, where Chika awaited.

"Go all the way," he said.

In place of a reply, Saraya offered his right hand.

Ninagawa gripped it.

It was a cold hand.

Chapter 1

A Hundred Twenty Million People

1

That day, starting before dawn, a ripple of shock went through all of Japan.

There were giant ad spreads in all three of the major national newspapers.

The advertisement commissioned a murder.

There weren't many faces in the Security Section office on the sixteenth floor of MPD HQ when Kazuki Mekari showed up. After exchanging greetings with a few colleagues, he headed to his desk.

"Mr. Mekari, did you see it?" called out a junior of his, Atsushi Shiraiwa, who'd arrived in the office before him.

Mekari wasn't quite sure what "it" meant.

Shiraiwa extracted a newspaper from his bag.

"This! It's insane," he said like some brat even though he was almost thirty.

He was a pretty decent guy overall, but his immaturity as an agent of the law and as a man was evident.

Putting aside Mekari's own issues, that is.

He was shown the ad spread in the morning edition. Mekari

didn't subscribe to the morning paper at home because he usually read it in this very room.

"PLEASE KILL THIS MAN"

The ridiculously large bold text danced before his eyes. Beneath was a large portrait of a male face labeled "Kunihide Kiyomaru, Age 34." After that, "As Thanks, Will Pay One Billion Yen," followed by a signature, "Takaoki Ninagawa," then a website url, a mobile url, and a free-dial phone number.

That was all there was to the ad.

Visit us on our website for more information, so to speak.

Despite the fact that it was commissioning a murder, the ad didn't feel creepy, but was rather streamlined, with a modern feel. It had quite a lot of visual impact. A considerably skilled designer must have been hired for the purpose.

Without even having to visit the homepage, Mekari remembered.

Three months ago, a certain case had shocked the nation.

An elementary school girl had been murdered in the city. In no time Kiyomaru was fingered as the culprit. Apparently his DNA matched that left on the victim. He'd been arrested for committing a similar crime seven years ago and had only recently been released. Although he was wanted nationwide, he had yet to be apprehended.

What stunned everyone wasn't the nature of the case itself, but rather the fact that the victim was Takaoki Ninagawa's granddaughter.

Takaoki Ninagawa was the biggest fish of all the big fish in Japan's corporate world, a prominent success figure whose name was familiar to any grownup. His speech and demeanor hinted at a no-nonsense personality.

His fortune was rumored to be in the dozens of billions, possibly over a hundred billion yen.

"On TV too, it's been the talk all morning."

Shiraiwa seemed to be enjoying it all as a bit of entertainment.

How stupid… That was Mekari's impression of the ad.

He understood not letting your granddaughter's murder go. Even if Kiyomaru was arrested, there was no knowing how much of a punishment he would receive. Although this was his second murder, he'd already served time for his first crime, and even with the recidivism, Mekari wasn't sure Kiyomaru would be slapped with a life sentence. Either way, it seemed likely that he'd enter society again in around a decade.

Of course the bereaved would be furious.

The current legal system wasn't designed to appease the victim side's thirst for retribution. Yet, if revenge was the goal, there had to be other ways. The bounty just seemed to be making a spectacle of Ninagawa's rage. At least, Mekari thought so.

What was more confusing was the ad making it onto the leading newspapers.

From what Shiraiwa had gathered from TV, the bounty had made it onto every regional edition of the three major newspapers. But there was no way such an ad could have made it past the companies' ad inspectors. It wasn't even a matter of inspecting. It was only natural to assume that the plates had been swapped out immediately before printing.

Yet there was no way bribing one staffer at the printers could have achieved this. There should have been plenty of people involved throughout the various stages. There also had to be personnel in charge of final checks before the printings were shipped out.

How many people did you need to have in your pocket to achieve such a thing?

They would eventually be arrested, not to mention fired. How much of a bribe was enough to convince people to forget their jobs and become accomplices in such a crime?

Mekari didn't even have a guess as to the sum Ninagawa must have spent just to put out the ad.

Perhaps Takaoki Ninagawa had already gone mad, he suspected.

As usual, Shiraiwa began to study for the promotion exam to become an assistant inspector. It wasn't something you did while on duty, but no one reprimanded him for it.

Both Mekari and Shiraiwa were SPs with the mobile contingent of the MPD Security Section. The SPs, or security police, were in charge of protecting VIPs, which included the Prime Minister and each cabinet member, the speakers of both houses of the Diet, the chief of the Supreme Court, the leaders of each political party, the Governor of Tokyo, and the chairman of the Federation of Economic Organizations. The mobile contingent, however, had no set beat.

The Mobile Security Subsection was called upon for large-scale escort operations such as when the President of the United States visited Japan, or when the SPs charged with protecting specific targets were unavailable for duty for any reason. They were the reserve unit, and as such, their customary duty was to be on standby. Every day, endlessly on standby.

At Shiraiwa's age, Mekari, too, had spent all of his time studying for the promotion exam.

He'd made assistant inspector when he was thirty-one. Mekari was now thirty-eight.

Three years had passed since he'd lost any desire to be promoted.

Like any other day, he decided to take lunch at the cafeteria in the building.

On the TV was some chimera of a program that was neither straight news nor a variety show. Unsurprisingly, the topic was the bounty in the morning papers.

Mekari began eating the daily special as he watched. The people in charge at the newspapers' printing departments were apparently being questioned by the police. The public relations rep of one of the companies was just repeating "I don't know" and "It's under investigation" to the interviewer.

It had already been announced that Takaoki Ninagawa was currently an inpatient at a university hospital in Tokyo and that no visitors were allowed. According to the hospital, it was unable to disclose details pertaining to his condition. An immense press crowd was visible behind the reporter who relayed this from in front of the hospital.

The program went on to discuss the website. The Kiyo-maru Site, as it was called, was apparently gaining hits at an exponential rate. Multiple websites with the same content seemed to be linked together so that no matter how many people accessed it at once, it still loaded in a blink.

According to the site, the condition for receiving the one billion yen reward for killing Kiyomaru was:

1. To receive a guilty verdict for a murder or manslaughter charge against Kunihide Kiyomaru (multiple persons possible).

2. To be publicly recognized as being responsible for the death of Kunihide Kiyomaru (multiple persons possible).

According to the site, no matter how many people met the requirements, each person would still be paid one billion yen.

Such largesse, Mekari thought. There really was no such thing as stinginess at Ninagawa's level of wealth.

Even so, although requirement one couldn't be any clearer, Mekari didn't really get what kind of situation requirement two was referring to. Maybe it was accounting for self-defense or emergency evacuation conditions? Maybe assisted suicide? Either way, it seemed highly unlikely.

In addition, an exclusive phone number for responding to any questions had been posted. Apparently, like the website, it never kept any caller waiting. An entire army of operators had to be on standby.

How polite and generous.

On the program, guests including a prosecutor turned lawyer, a crim law scholar, and a former head of MPD's Investigation Section One were offering legal analyses as well as predictions on future developments. Another commentator, a writer, was spewing criticism in a bit of a frenzy.

Despite the incredible event—a newspaper ad calling upon the general public to murder someone—the TV proceedings, Mekari mused, were following the same old mundane pattern.

As he left the cafeteria and headed back up to the sixteenth floor, someone called out, "Hey."

The man had been in the same year as Mekari at the police academy and now served as a plainclothes in Investigation Section One. Mekari didn't even have time to return his greeting before the man dove in.

"Seriously, what a hassle. I'm not even in charge of the Kiyomaru case but they're mobilizing me anyway, the brass want us to crush the site asap, turns out the provider's location is some little island country in the South Pacific, there's nothing we can really do..."

After finishing the one-way conversation, he said, "See ya," and left.

Mekari raised his hand, but no one was around to see.

At any rate, the Ninagawa camp's operation was flawless. They had no doubt been preparing meticulously for some time.

Something bothered Mekari, though. Why was a man in charge of violent crimes, at Section One, being ordered to go squash a website? True, it was relevant to a murder case for which a special headquarters was still in place, but it seemed odd that Sec One, the poster boys of the MPD, was going after something like an illegal newspaper ad and a website with socially unacceptable content. Wasn't the violent crimes section supposed to come on stage after Kunihide Kiyomaru's corpse turned up in the

Metropolitan Police's jurisdiction?

The MPD had four criminal investigation subdivisions. Sec Two was in charge of "intellectual" wrongdoing such as fraud, bribery, and electoral irregularities. Sec Three attended to larceny cases like theft, pickpocketing, and currency forgery. Sec Four, nicknamed *Marubo*, handled organizations that resorted to force, namely the yakuza.

Sec One was for investigating violent crimes such as murder and assault; robberies, including rape; arson; and special cases like kidnappings, hostage situations, corporate blackmail, hijackings, and bombings.

Whichever subdivision or station ended up dealing with the case, Takaoki Ninagawa was the ringleader and his whereabouts were known. Mekari believed it should be a cake walk.

He wondered even after returning to Security Sec. If nothing else, he had plenty of time.

Although the MPD were the police of the capital, in the end they were a municipal department. The National Police Agency that stood over all of the prefectural forces was the true federal organization.

The murder perpetrated by Kiyomaru had happened within the MPD's jurisdiction, but didn't Ninagawa's nationwide bounty shift the burden to the National Police Agency?

The NPA itself didn't have any investigative muscle. It was a huge bureaucracy.

Trust in the police force had to be protected as part of governance.

What if some fool, blinded by greed at Ninagawa's offer of one billion yen, actually killed Kiyomaru? It would indicate that putting a bounty on a suspect's head was more effective than leaving it to the police. The force's authority would plummet.

Kiyomaru had to be arrested before he was killed, no matter what. Perhaps, at the NPA's urging, MPD Sec One was going all in too.

That, however, was nothing more than a guess on Mekari's part. In the first place, who could kill Kiyomaru when he'd evaded the police's search net for three months?

Not that it particularly mattered to an SP like Mekari.

He left the office at his usual time.

Mekari's home was in Suginami Ward.

Upon getting married, he'd left his state-owned quarters to live in a civilian apartment building. Although the former was more affordable, ranks ended up affecting neighborhood relationships, and he'd heard that many wives of policemen had a hard time of it. He hadn't wanted to put his wife through unnecessary stress.

"I'm pretty thick, so I'll be fine!"

His wife had said so with a laugh, but she'd seemed to enjoy her relaxed apartment life just fine.

He'd almost forgotten, but today was his wife's birthday. He'd been aware of it for several days now but hadn't done anything in particular like buy a present.

They'd gotten married eleven years ago. He didn't feel like he needed to do anything special at this stage, but he also didn't want her to think he'd forgotten. Maybe he needed to buy her something on the way back.

But if he brought home a birthday cake, he knew he wouldn't be able to finish it on his own.

Might lighting more incense than usual suffice?

Mekari smiled sadly.

2

Mekari got home at slightly past 8:00 p.m.

He'd dined at the food stop in front of the train station and visited the pharmacy to buy shampoo. Then he'd dropped by a traditional confectionary store close to his home and purchased three mugwort *dango* balls, his wife's favorite.

Putting his bag down, he opened the pack and rummaged around in his cabinet for a plate. It was his wife's birthday, so he was going the extra mile.

He placed the plate with the sweets on his wife's altar and lit the usual number of incense sticks.

He tried to say something to the portrait of his deceased wife, but he thought it'd be odd to wish her a happy birthday.

Did the dead even care about birthdays? Or was the date of death the only one with any meaning for them?

But why not celebrate this day, when thirty years ago, she'd entered this world?

Mekari just went ahead with it.

He vaguely recalled doing the same thing the previous year,

and the year before.

"Happy birthday," he said out loud.

And please take care of me from now on too, he added silently.

Mekari's wife had died three years ago, of esophageal cancer.

It was too late by the time they found out. The cancer progressed quickly in young people. His wife rapidly withered away.

The doctor told them that if she had surgery, it would only steal what strength she had left. They were told the same thing at every hospital they visited.

His wife realized that she was doomed. When she asked Mekari point-blank, he didn't lie to her.

The two of them cried together.

I don't want to die, she said, weeping half for his sake. *I don't want to leave you alone.*

Death was merciless. To the dying, and to those who would be left behind.

At that time, Mekari was assigned to the Prime Minister.

Six SP were usually assigned to the premier, and Mekari had been chosen as one of those six. It wasn't exactly an exhausting job, but it kept him busy day after day. It wasn't the kind of beat that allowed him to go home every night.

When the head of the Security Section got wind of it, he transferred Mekari to the mobile contingent. Thanks to that, Mekari was able to spend a sufficient amount of time at his wife's side.

They went on vacation two times while she could still walk. Hokkaido in the summer and Okinawa in the winter. They'd chosen the two far edges of Japan.

His wife wrote him numerous memos so that after her death, he wouldn't struggle to take care of himself.

By now, Mekari had them memorized.

As he was about to leave her altar, a thought occurred to him.

"I dunno about serving *dango* without tea."

It was as if his wife had spoken to him.

All right, all right.

Turning on the television in the dining room, he entered the kitchen. He filled the kettle with water and put it on the stove. It was a bit tedious that he had to start by boiling some water.

It's not like you're actually gonna take a sip.

On TV, a clever-looking comedian and a dumb-looking one were insulting each other.

Mekari tried changing the channel, but the other stations didn't have anything that caught his interest either.

Even so, he kept it on.

Because the sound was important to people who lived alone.

Opening the tea caddy, he noticed that there was only a little left, but it would do for tonight. He saw his wife's teacup for the first time in a while and felt a bit lonesome.

On TV, a crying kindergarten boy chased around a celebrity who wore a demon costume.

Mekari wondered what it would have been like if he and his wife had had a child. Perhaps she'd have regretted her illness only the more. He didn't think he could take proper care of kids by himself and most likely would have had his wife's parents take them in and raise them. Even so…

Even so, someone whom Mekari could talk to about his wife to share his loss seemed like a beautiful thing.

His wife's hometown was in Chiba. Both of her parents were still alive and well, although Mekari had not seen them since the second anniversary of her death.

Mekari himself didn't have a family to go back to.

His mother passed away in a traffic accident when he was in his second year of middle school. Later, his father remarried and started a new family, taking on three elementary school kids.

Shortly before that, Mekari left with his little sister. It was the year he entered college. During his four years there, he and his sister lived together, just the two of them.

He became a police officer, and around when he transferred to the MPD dormitory, his little sister suddenly married an American. They lived in Los Angeles now.

Mekari hadn't really had anywhere to call home since his mother's death.

When he married, he gained more than just a wife but a home.

He didn't have anywhere to return to but here.

Placing the freshly made tea on the altar, he returned to the dining room. A short news segment was playing in the break between shows.

The Chief Cabinet Secretary was fielding questions about Ninagawa's newspaper ad at a regular press conference.

Mekari took the cup of tea he'd poured for himself and settled in front of the TV.

"Well, you know, Japan has such a thing called the rule of law, and this isn't permissible. At any rate, I doubt any of our citizens would stoop so low as to take this seriously," the Chief Cabinet Secretary answered, sounding as sarcastic as ever.

He seemed to be going out of his way to brush off the case and to give the nation the impression that the bounty was an unrealistic fantasy.

Could Ninagawa's newspaper ad really—no, the ad itself was nothing more than bait to rile up the huge media platform called the tee-vee.

Would any citizens take Ninagawa's bounty seriously?

Yes.

In fact, it might be more difficult to find ones who didn't.

Mekari had come to think so.

Ninagawa was going all the way. At least, Mekari doubted anyone still questioned it.

Then, would anyone actually try to kill Kiyomaru for the one billion?

Yes.

And there had to be a good number of them.

The world had no shortage of people who murdered innocents for chump change.

In one case, a man who'd wanted more money to squander started out by killing an unsuspecting acquaintance. For a measly five thousand yen.

In another case, a man had searched online for someone willing to kill his wife. He wanted the insurance money. A fellow who accepted the job for thirty million yen was arrested for trying to murder a woman he'd never met before.

How idiotic. Yet such idiots were a dime a dozen.

If the reward money was one billion yen, the idiots would multiply without end.

One billion yen. It was an absurd amount of money for an individual. Winning the highest prize at the lottery three times in a row still fell short of the sum.

There were most certainly people who did anything for money. They didn't bat an eye at murder or life in prison.

Ever since the new anti-organized crime law, yakuza who could no longer pay their dues were said to be on the rise. Former gangsters, who, in effect, had been laid off, were perpetrating truly heinous crimes. There were more such cases than one cared to count.

For yakuza, penal servitude was nothing more than an extended business trip. If killing a single man and spending seven or eight years behind bars could net one billion yen, then no other gig paid so well.

Robberies involving guns were also increasing every year. There were plenty of unresolved cases, but the robbed cash was dozens of millions of yen at most.

Would those perps hesitate to harm a man with a billion-yen bounty on his head who happened to pass by?

In addition, in recent years there had been a surge in crimes committed by foreigners. Unlike regular aliens working away from home, these folks entered the country clearly intending to rake it in through illegal means. The vast majority of them had military experience as well as criminal records back in their home countries. Apparently, quite a few of them thought nothing of murder. If those types managed to acquire one billion yen, they'd live like kings after repatriating.

Apart from crooks interested in money, there were people who didn't think twice about taking lives.

Parents who slew their children. Every day, the news showed cases of infant abuse. People who threw a baby at a wall, killing it because its wailing was annoying, were beyond comprehension. If you offered one billion to them, wouldn't they gladly hurl a stranger's kid at a wall too? Even themselves?

There was no end, either, to violent incidents committed by minors. A supposedly good boy, usually quiet and with no delinquency record, suddenly severs the head of an elementary school kid. Another hijacks a highway bus and kills the passengers. Yet another shoves a toddler off the roof of a high rise for no particular reason.

All actual cases with unclear motives. Whether there even was a motive was debatable. Perhaps it had been nothing more than a game to them. Perhaps they'd despaired at their daily mundane lives. Perhaps they were filled with loathing for a world controlled by adults.

What would such kids make of prey like Kiyomaru?

When Mekari glanced back up, the TV was playing a serial drama. Pretty-faced flight crew and cabin attendants were facing some kind of crisis.

Mekari decided to go take a bath.

He started to fill the tub with hot water and showered, taking his time.

Today he could finally wash his hair with shampoo again. The past few times he'd used body soap, so his hair had felt squeaky afterwards and uncomfortably rough even after drying.

It wasn't that he hadn't gone to buy some. The product he wanted had been sold out. Rather than wash his hair with body soap, he could have bought a different brand of shampoo. Most people would have. Mekari, however, couldn't.

He didn't want to use any brand other than the one his wife had picked out for him.

His life with her wasn't open to change. Continuing to protect the details was Mekari's tiny show of defiance. If possible, minus his wife, he wanted to keep everything else exactly the way it had been.

Would others find him strange?

If so he wanted to ask them: *It's just shampoo and I'll use the kind I want, what's your goddamn problem?*

A year after he had lost his wife, Mekari had been invited out to drink with the head of the Mobile Security Subsection, Inspector Ohki.

Ohki inviting out an underling was unheard of. The man's straight-lacedness was his main redeeming trait, and the word was that he rarely imbibed. He usually addressed his subordinates in a curt manner, but perhaps because he was drunk, he started playing the big brother with Mekari.

"Hey, if you don't cut yourself loose of the dead, you won't find happiness…"

I don't want to find happiness, sir, Mekari had replied silently.

By the time he'd finished bathing, the ten o'clock news program had begun. It was giving a breakdown of the two crimes Kiyomaru had committed: Megumi Nishino's murder seven years ago and Chika Ninagawa's murder three months ago.

The screen showed a close-up of Megumi's face. Her innocent smile pierced Mekari's heart.

Chika's photograph appeared to be from a field meet. She was laughing embarrassedly with a red headband.

Megumi had been six, Chika seven. The fact that there were men who saw such little girls as sexual objects was incomprehensible to Mekari.

Both incidents were almost unbearably gruesome.

Beaten relentlessly before being killed, the two girls had been left with barely any front teeth. Their faces had swollen up to the point of being unidentifiable, and they'd bled from both ears. A piece of Megumi's shattered lower jaw bone had rammed into her upper jaw.

Kiyomaru's face was displayed next. It was a different photo from the one in the ad. He looked skinny and seedy and his eyes oozed malice.

I could kill this man, Mekari thought. No, he actually wanted to kill the man.

Many of the show's viewers had to be feeling the same way.

Whether they would actually do it was a different matter.

Mekari recalled that thirty thousand Japanese supposedly killed themselves every year. They said Japan had an exceedingly high suicide rate compared to other nations.

Many of those people were middle-aged or above. Laid-off salarymen and owners of small businesses in dire straits turned their hopes to their insurance money saving their families and hanged themselves. It wouldn't be strange at all if such well-intentioned ordinary citizens, who planned to die anyway, saw fit to kill Kiyomaru to leave a billion yen for their loved ones.

Suddenly, there was a commotion at the studio. The nervous female newscaster began to read a script that had been handed to her.

"Just now, at around 9:15 p.m., suspect Kunihide Kiyomaru turned himself in to Fukuoka South Station of the Fukuoka Prefectural Police."

Ah, Mekari thought. *The ad also had this in mind.*

A standard cash award for information wouldn't have riled up the media. The ceaseless coverage had convinced Kiyomaru that his time was up.

Just then, Mekari's home phone rang. It was Subsection Chief Ohki.

"I'm sorry this is so sudden, but you'll be flying out to Fukuoka tomorrow."

Why?!

3

Mekari stood before the desk of the chief of the Security Section.

Subsection Chief Ohki had told him on the phone the previous night to report to the Section Chief first thing in the morning.

Shiraiwa stood next to Mekari.

"I'm sure you're already aware, but last night, Kiyomaru turned himself in to the Fukuoka Police. In order to get him to the prosecutors, he needs to be transferred to the MPD without delay."

Starting at the beginning, the Section Chief repeated everything that Ohki had already told Mekari.

"Under ordinary circumstances, personnel from the special investigation headquarters would take Kiyomaru in, but this case is anomalous."

Ninagawa's peculiar classified ad had been taken up by media around the world, and the National Police Agency was blowing a fuse—*It's a challenge to the authority of the state!*

"We don't know the extent of the ad's effect, but we must be prepared for a potentially dangerous transfer. And so, following a proposal from the director, we're taking the irregular measure of assigning SP to Kiyomaru."

Mekari's first mission in a while didn't involve a VIP. Of all things, he'd be serving as a bodyguard for human trash.

Two SPs was the norm for personal escorts, with the exception of the Prime Minister who was assigned six. In other words, they were granting a ruthless murderer VIP treatment using taxpayer money.

Old Ninagawa sure was causing them trouble.

There was no mistaking that the mission was riskier than a routine escort. Perhaps Mekari and Shiraiwa had been chosen because they were both single.

"Two guys from the special investigation HQ, one from the Fukuoka Police, and you two, a total of five personnel will form the transfer team. Get the details from Ohki. Just be aware that the nation's eyes and ears are glued to this case. Devote everything to the mission and bring honor to the MPD Security Section. That is all."

Having said his bit, the promotion-tracked Section Chief turned his attention back to the forms on his desk as if to warn that he no longer had any business with them.

"I guess the Chief didn't want to have to say it himself and shoved it on to me," Ohki complained with a wry smile. "See, by order of the Director-General of the National Police Agency, you're to treat this as an SS mission…"

The Secret Service, the security unit of the President of the United States. Though modeled after the SS, the Japanese SP's escorting style was distinctively unlike America's, where ordinary citizens could carry firearms.

"In short, shoot anyone who makes suspicious moves."

Like the Self-Defense Force, the Japanese security police abided by a policy of nonaggression. Although "proficiency with handguns: advanced or higher" was a factor in eligibility for the SP, since its establishment not a single member had fired a shot in the line of duty.

This time, they were to "shoot anyone who makes suspicious moves." Responding after an attack was too late. The Director-General clearly felt this was a crisis.

While the Chief would never explicitly defy him, perhaps "bring honor to the MPD Security Section" meant "protect the charge without firing a shot" in order to uphold the pride of the Japanese SP.

Or perhaps, as an elite who'd joined the National Police Agency and was on loan to the MPD, the legend of "zero shots fired since establishment" crumbling during his brief tenure as the section chief was too much of a stain on his resume.

"Well, I understand if you guys don't dig Kiyomaru being your charge, but think of it as safeguarding the force itself rather than a criminal."

By the time Mekari and Shiraiwa entered the Equipment Section, their loadout had been prepared by the staff.

Routine gear like bullet-proof vests, wireless radios, and special batons were stored within the Security Section. What the Equipment Section had ready for this mission was guns and ammo, along with holsters to carry them.

On regular duty, an SP bore a SIG P230, a mid-sized automatic handgun. The MPD's standard issue, the .380-caliber firearm was manufactured domestically on a license from the Swiss SIG company.

For this mission, however, they were being supplied with SIG P228s. The 9 mm compact pistol was an upgraded version of the SIG P220, the large automatic handgun used by the Self-Defense Force.

Special force outfits across the globe carried the P226, which came with a double-row magazine that fired more shots than the P220-1, itself a mod of the P220 that improved operability. The P228 trimmed down the barrel and grip of the P226 so that it was more compact and easier to hide underneath clothing. It was the gun used by the Secret Service.

Its capacity was thirteen plus one bullets. Compared to the P230's seven plus one, it could fire almost twice as many consecutive shots.

Its 9 mm x 19 ammo, nicknamed the 9 mm Parabellum, or 9 mm Luger, was almost the same diameter as the .380 ACP bullet used by the P230, but held more gunpowder and had the reputation of being the top anti-personnel choice.

Moreover, for this mission they had been provided with Silvertips.

Mekari was honestly quite surprised.

A product of the Winchester Company, the Silvertip had a coat of aluminum on a hole bored through the tip. It was a so-called dum-dum bullet.

While a gun's power was often attributed to its caliber and amount of gunpowder, the material and shape of the bullethead also had much to do with it. That power came in two forms: penetration and damage. The more the bullet was able to maintain its shape after contacting the target, the greater the penetration and the lesser the damage. In other words, for more damage, you had to make it easier for the bullet to deform.

Dum-dum bullets, designed to deform easily to heighten damage, mushroomed upon contact with the human body so that most of the kinetic energy went to destroying living tissue. Extremely lethal, they'd been banned for military use as being inhumane after the 1899 Hague Convention.

Among the dum-dum bullets were soft points, which exposed the soft lead core for easier expansion, and hollow points, which featured holes in the tip to magnify the effect.

The Silvertip, a hollow point, was special in that it controlled the timing of the expansion. Rather than deforming the moment it hit a target, it penetrated deep into the body before the exposed lead core mushroomed. For that reason, Silvertips were not sold to the public and were manufactured primarily for government use in America.

So why were these bullets, said to be so lethal, utilized by American agents of the law? Why were they being made available to Mekari and Shiraiwa for this mission?

It was to prevent the bullet from punching through the target and doing harm to blameless, ordinary citizens. Enhanced damage also meant reduced penetration.

In Japan, police rarely fired. When they did, it was almost always as a warning shot, and in general, officers carried firearms only to deter.

As a result, what happened when a bullet was fired into something as soft as a human body didn't receive sufficient attention. Shooting out the tires of a vehicle to stop a criminal from escaping seemed to be the eventuality in mind. Hence the same full-metal-jacket ammo as the military.

The FMJ was entirely encased in copper to make it more difficult for the lead cap to expand. This limited the damage to the human body since the bullet penetrated with a minimal loss of kinetic energy.

It seemed to be considered the humane choice in Japan. In America, however, that description belonged to ammo that didn't punch through to injure innocent citizens and that properly stopped within the body of a dangerous criminal who'd drawn fire from the police.

In this mission, they didn't know when, where, and who would emerge to attack Kiyomaru. If a man with a gun suddenly jumped out of a large crowd of curious onlookers, there was certainly no way they could shoot him with a highly penetrative bullet.

Mekari opened the Winchester paper carton containing fifty 9 mm bullets. They lay with their detonaters up, but one row of five shots was missing. Someone from the Equipment Section had no doubt fired some test shots to check for faulty merchandise.

He picked up one bullet. The gold-colored brass casing had a tip that gleamed silver, in which was bored a deep hole. Around the hole were several shallow grooves.

Mekari knew about the bullet, but this was his first time actually encountering one. He felt like he'd just seen something terribly ominous.

"This is crazy. It kinda feels like a Hollywood movie!" Shiraiwa babbled, completely at ease.

He's not a bad guy, Mekari tried to convince himself.

Being told to shoot suspicious persons with this bullet was almost synonymous to being told to kill suspicious persons.

Whether they could manage to was a different matter altogether.

He decided he'd have lunch with Shiraiwa that day. In the station's cafeteria, the TV was playing the same show.

Mekari ordered the special as usual. Today was fried horse mackerel and mapo tofu. Shiraiwa got curry rice. He always seemed to be eating curry.

"Is the curry here really that good?"

"Well, to be honest it's pretty bad."

Yeah, the guy was an idiot.

The TV conveyed information related to Kiyomaru as if nothing were more natural. Not many details had been available last night, but by now they had a better grasp of the situation.

When Kiyomaru turned himself in to Fukuoka South Station, apparently he was covered in blood.

He'd been sheltered by a man he'd met during his time in prison. The man was the leader of a crime group in Fukuoka that used illegal Chinese immigrants. Kiyomaru had been helping his business in exchange for shelter. Apparently he'd been promised help to escape the country when the time was right.

Thanks to Ninagawa's bounty, however, the man who'd protected him suddenly tried to kill him. Striking back in desperation, Kiyomaru grabbed his opponent's knife and stabbed him. Kiyomaru had been drenched by the resulting spurt of blood, but he himself only had minor injuries.

Although he somehow managed to escape, he had nowhere to go. He couldn't even change his blood-soaked clothes. He knew that he would eventually be found and killed by someone. After considering the alternative, he turned himself in to the police.

The report was streamed from in front of the Fukuoka South Police Station. A few hundred ordinary citizens appeared to have gathered in the vicinity. Soon after it was broadcast that Kiyomaru had turned himself in, a map of the area around the police station and details of the building had been posted on the Kiyomaru Site. It was highly doubtful that anyone would be stupid enough to attack a police station, and most of the civilians were probably just there hoping something exciting would happen, but the mood was fairly foreboding.

"You know how the Subsection Chief told us to 'shoot anyone who makes suspicious moves'? How suspicious do you suppose they have to be before we can shoot them?"

"Shoot if they're suspicious enough that you think you have to shoot," Mekari enlightened Shiraiwa.

"But like, if someone among the onlookers suddenly sticks his hand in his bag, it's suspicious, but he could be pulling out a camera or binoculars, you know?"

"If someone sticks his hand into his bag, pull out your gun. If he pulls out a gun, shoot. If he pulls out binoculars, don't shoot."

"But would I make the shot in time that way?"

"Make sure, even so."

The screen changed to show the Minister of Justice's press conference.

A former police bureaucrat, the current Minister of Justice was in high spirits. He urged citizens to remain calm in the face of

Ninagawa's bounty and went on to use far too many words to say, *The dignity of our nation is on the line, and we will not forgive anyone who acts in such a violent manner. We won't let Kiyomaru be killed no matter what.*

As they exited the cafeteria, they passed a colleague from Security Sec.

"Congrats, guys, you've just become the men closest to the one billion yen."

The colleague laughed and walked away.

What a shallow joke. But even though it was a joke, was Mekari the only one who thought the man's eyes were tinged with envy?

Well, it wasn't like Shiraiwa would have noticed... He was Shiraiwa, after all.

At exactly one in the afternoon, Mekari and Shiraiwa entered the office of the head of the Investigation Department.

The guys from Investigation Section One arrived only a moment behind them.

An administrator from Sec One introduced the two investigators who would be joining the team: Assistant Inspector Takeshi Okumura and Sergeant Masataka Kanbashi.

Mekari had seen Okumura around before. He was an old Sec One hand, and Mekari had heard that he was very reliable. He looked to be in his mid-fifties. His calm visage was less veteran cop than credit union branch manager.

Kanbashi, in his mid-thirties, could have been the bad cop from some TV drama.

After Mekari and Shiraiwa introduced themselves, Okumura said, "Looking forward to working with you," while Kanbashi didn't open his mouth and just nodded.

That was when the head of the Investigation Department made his appearance.

It was rumored that he'd make MPD Commissioner or NPA Director-General one day.

"The National Police Agency is currently looking into possible methods for transporting Kiyomaru. When you gentlemen arrive in Fukuoka, follow the instructions of the folks from the Kyushu Jurisdiction Police Division. Because this type of transfer is unprecedented, we should be prepared for the worst. Be prepared to face all one hundred twenty million of our citizens as your enemies as you execute this mission."

Staring into the faces of each transfer team member in turn, he spoke again.

"Make sure to bring Kiyomaru back alive!"

He hadn't told Mekari and the others to come back alive.

4

The four team members who exited MPD HQ split up into two taxis and headed for Haneda Airport.

Mekari felt groggy because he hadn't slept very well after the call from Subsection Chief Ohki. He wanted to catch some shut-eye in the brief time on their way to the airport, but Shiraiwa wouldn't let him.

"That Kanbashi guy, doesn't he fit the 'bad cop' stereotype like totally?"

Mekari laughed. So Shiraiwa had thought the same thing.

For a cop, Kanbashi didn't look particularly buff. It wasn't even that his face was scary. He just seemed uncouth and rough.

"When I was a newbie and stationed at Mitaka, there was a guy who was sorta like that in Subsec One. They really feel similar... That guy ended up robbing a loan shark and was arrested."

Mekari couldn't help but laugh again.

Robbing a loan shark suited Kanbashi better than wearing the badge. At the same time, he felt a bit annoyed that he'd laughed at one of Shiraiwa's comments.

"Mr. Mekari, what do you think of this mission?" Shiraiwa suddenly asked, his expression turning serious.

"Nothing in particular. It's just a normal job."

"This is normal? I mean, it's Kiyomaru."

"Is he not good enough for you?"

"I'm not really that eager to protect him, to be honest..."

"I hated the Prime Minister, too."

"Maybe you did, but this one's a criminal..."

"Who's to say our citizens don't see politicians as worse crooks?"

"Well, even then..."

"My point is that it doesn't matter who our charge is. If the brass tell us to protect whomever, we protect him. That's our job, isn't it..."

"Mr. Mekari, aren't you interested in the one billion?"

"Not at all."

"Seriously? Why aren't you interested?"

"Well, are you thinking of killing Kiyomaru?"

"Of course not! Sure, one billion sounds tempting, but I kinda doubt money made off of murder could bring me happiness…"

"What? You're looking for happiness? You have cute dreams, like an office lady…"

"Of course everyone wants to find happiness!"

"Then quit being an SP and go for the one billion. You can be happy then, huh?"

"But if I kill someone, I doubt I'll ever find a decent wife…"

"Idiot. If you've got a billion, you'll have all the girls you want."

"I don't want a wife who's after my money! Could you love a woman who's okay with a murderer so long as he's rich?"

"I guess you have a point…"

Such a thing hadn't even occurred to Mekari. Although he, too, was single now, taking another wife was far from his mind. He supposed he'd be lonely living alone for the rest of his life. But it wouldn't be because he didn't remarry. He was lonely because she was gone.

Mekari felt like his wife was always watching him. A constant gaze, from a little behind and above him.

There was no way he could do anything that would make his wife's smile fade.

Their All Nippon Airways flight was scheduled to depart at 3:15 p.m. The four of them arrived at the airport approximately an hour before departure and finished checking in.

They surrendered a case containing their security gear, but the same couldn't be done with their guns and ammo. In the off chance that a customer accidentally took their luggage upon arrival, there'd be hell to pay. At the same time, they couldn't leave their heat with the airport staff like with knives and scissors. Police firearms could not be passed into civilian hands no matter what.

Even if the police were armed for official business, they were not allowed to board civilian passenger planes with firearms on their person. When the need arose, the airline company provided a duralumin case into which the guns and ammo were locked. The keys were kept with the airline company, and the case was carried into the aircraft by the cops themselves. This way the weapons remained with them at all times, but the case couldn't be opened in the aircraft. Upon landing at the destination airport, staff unlocked the case and removed the belongings. That was how they did things.

Shiraiwa took the yellow duralumin case with a sticker that read "TOKYO P.D." The case contained two two-inch New Nambu M60 revolvers containing five rounds of .38 special bullets, two SIG P228s loaded with fourteen 9 mm x 19 bullets, and four spare magazines with thirteen 9 mm x 19 bullets each.

Okumura bought a two thousand-yen box of sweet bean jelly to present as a gift to the local police. They still had forty minutes until departure and decided to kill some time at a cafe restaurant. All four of them ordered coffee. Mekari was afraid that Shiraiwa might order curry, but thankfully that didn't happen.

"But seriously, you guys have it rough. To have to act as a shield for scum like Kiyomaru," Kanbashi said to Mekari and Shiraiwa. There was some bite to his words.

Perhaps he hadn't meant anything by it, and it was just the way he spoke. He certainly seemed the type.

Shiraiwa, however, seemed irked.

"It doesn't matter who. We protect whomever we're told to protect. It's our job," he replied bluntly, repeating what he'd just been told by Mekari without a hint of shame.

"But is a guy like that worth protecting? A perverted freak who rapes and murders a seven-year-old girl."

Shiraiwa seemed at a loss for words, so Mekari answered in his place.

"It's not our place to judge a person's worth…"

This from someone who outranked him gave Kanbashi no choice but to shut up.

"Mekari, what kind of attacks does the Security Section have in mind?" Okumura changed the topic.

"None. After all, this case is unprecedented… But as just a personal opinion, I believe Takaoki Ninagawa was serious when he placed that bounty. I don't think the ad is all he has up his sleeve."

"True, Ninagawa seems very serious about this…" agreed Okumura, his face grim.

Kanbashi also nodded. "According to a journo, it's being rumored in political circles that cash by the billions has been showered on force brass and the ruling party's Diet members. They're saying old man Ninagawa's planning on using up his whole multi-hundred-billion-yen fortune..."

Mekari thought that was more than possible, even if it was some newspaper reporter on the police beat taking a guess.

Shiraiwa voiced a very Shiraiwa-esque doubt. "But how many ordinary citizens would dare to attack despite a police escort?"

That was most certainly true. Very few would try to attack Kiyomaru.

But that was speaking of ordinary citizens.

On the plane too, Mekari and Shiraiwa ended up sitting next to each other. They didn't know where Okumura and Kanbashi were seated.

The public broadcaster's mid-day news began on the crystal-screen monitor up front. It showed a crowd of people gathered outside Fukuoka South Police Station. Mekari plugged in his headphones for the audio.

The government had released a comment that "It is legally impossible to receive a monetary reward for committing murder," warning citizens against being tempted by the foolish ad.

Both the visuals and audio suddenly cut out and switched to the flight safety instructions, so Mekari removed his headphones.

"Though they say it's legally impossible..." Shiraiwa started, having also removed his headphones. "Last night, I checked out the Kiyomaru Site on my computer. There was this endless list of answers that a team of legal pros had given to questions they'd received over their inquiry number, and man, they were super specific! There were questions like, won't the one billion be confiscated by the government? What about taxes? Can we specify who'll retrieve the money? And on the flip side, how do I prevent my family from stealing the money while I'm in prison? Or, since Ninagawa's old, is there still a guarantee that I'll be compensated if he passes away? It was all so thorough, and readers might think, 'Hey, maybe I can get that money'..."

"I see. But I want to sleep now, so can we cut the conversation here?"

"Oh! Sorry..."

"We don't know what'll happen over there, so try to get some sleep too."

Mekari closed his eyes.

As Shiraiwa suggested, the money would probably be paid out. Someone in Ninagawa's social position absolutely needed to follow through on a promise made in public. If people doubted it, no one would try to kill Kiyomaru. Ninagawa must have had experts on law research ways to find all the various legal loopholes before his camp had even begun. The government, of course, wanted such a contract to be null and void. But even an amateur like Mekari felt like there had to be a way.

For example, Ninagawa might announce his refusal to honor the bounty, so that the family of the person who killed Kiyomaru for one billion yen could launch a civil lawsuit. "My husband committed murder because of the ad. Ninagawa needs to pay damages," or something like that. Then, during the trial, they'd settle—for a monetary compensation of one billion yen. Faced with a settlement, the court wouldn't be able to lift a finger. It would clearly be a farce, but Mekari didn't see any legal issues.

Moreover, weren't damages tax-exempt?

Lost in thought, Mekari drifted to sleep.

The Fukuoka Airport spread to the east of Hakata Ward in Fukuoka City. Apparently it took around twenty minutes by car to get to the South Police Station, located in Shiobaru, South Ward.

When they exited Terminal 2, the taxi boarding area was directly outside. This time they decided to hail just one car. Okumura took the shotgun seat. The back seats felt crowded with three large men, but it couldn't be helped.

"Please take us to Fukuoka South Police Station," Okumura requested.

The middle-aged driver looked appalled. "You folks too? And so curious as to fly down here…" He turned around to glance at the back seat and froze even as he spoke, probably realizing that Mekari and the others weren't rubberneckers. Perhaps he mistook them for a gang of assassins come to kill Kiyomaru.

"We're from the Tokyo Metropolitan Police. We've come to escort Kiyomaru," Okumura disabused him with a pleasant smile.

"W-Well, I apologize for my rudeness…"

The driver pulled out, grimacing.

The taxi radio was playing a local commercial broadcast.

The male entertainer asked, "What would you do if you got one billion?"

His female counterpart answered, "I want to become like the Kardashians!" and exploded in laughter at her own joke. Soon after though, she said, "Oh, looks like some news just came in. It's all yours, Mr. Yamamoto from the news department!"

"Yes, we just received a report. Kunihide Kiyomaru, currently held in custody at Fukuoka South Police Station, was just attacked by an officer keeping watch and was wounded."

A shock ran through everyone in the cab.

"The officer who attacked suspect Kiyomaru was subdued by another officer on the scene and immediately placed under arrest for attempted murder. Suspect Kiyomaru was promptly transferred to the nearby Kyushu Central Hospital, but we have no details on the severity of his injuries…"

It had happened.

An officer had attacked Kiyomaru.

The thing that everyone had predicted but avoided saying out loud had happened at last.

There were approximately two hundred forty thousand police officers nationwide, and no end to their list of scandals.

Killing a co-ed. One's wife. A lover. Robbing a bank. A post office. A loan shark. Arson. Rape. Ganging up and beating someone up. Blindly spraying bullets. Police officers had been arrested for those crimes and countless others.

The force had a tendency to conceal such wrongdoings.

It was as bad as that just for the cases that ended up surfacing. If you included incidents pushed under the table, a scary number of personnel had broken the law. There were also station-wide crimes involving dubious seizures of firearms and fake receipts.

Some cops were mired in debt. Some committed suicide.

What would happen if Kiyomaru were exposed to such

personnel? Mekari felt something cold run down his spine.

Perhaps this was Ninagawa's goal from the very beginning. To first scare Kiyomaru out of hiding with the bounty, then to have an officer kill him.

The police had guns. The police had easy access to Kiyomaru.

Even after serving time for killing Kiyomaru, with one billion, you could start a new life.

Neither Okumura, nor Kanbashi, nor Shiraiwa, nor Mekari said a word.

At this point, nowhere was safe for Kiyomaru.

5

An incredible number of people flooded the area in front of Kyushu Central Hospital. The crowd from the police station must have followed Kiyomaru here. Numerous uniformed officers were out in the streets glaring at the onlookers, and the media were also there in droves.

Mekari and company's cab arrived while traffic police were trying to redirect vehicles. When it pulled up in front of the hospital, a uniformed officer came running in alarm.

Okumura lowered the shotgun seat window and opened a black double-folded case lengthwise, showing his police badge and identification. The officer saluted and let the taxi through.

When the four men got off in front of the main entrance, they were once again checked by an uniformed officer. Okumura presented his ID and asked the fellow to fill them in.

Apparently, Kiyomaru had been taken out of his cell for questioning by an officer, age 22, tasked with the detainment who pulled out a collapsible camping knife he'd brought from home. He'd stabbed at Kiyomaru, aiming for his chest, but Kiyomaru had bent his left arm and prevented the knife from finding his torso. The officer was immediately held down by other personnel, and his attack ended in failure.

The wound to Kiyomaru's left arm had been deep, and it had also bled heavily. For a time, he had gone into shock.

Mekari had a thought: If even one more officer on the scene had wanted to kill Kiyomaru, wouldn't the attempt have succeeded? Or perhaps if a gun had been used.

Detainment personnel didn't bear firearms. Hence the officer had to resort to bringing a knife, but his attempt was difficult to pull off alone. Of course, even with a gun, killing someone from a distance required consummate skill. If a person who could get into stabbing distance used a gun, however, success was a near certainty.

The four men thanked the uniform officer and entered the building.

As soon as they did, a man who looked to be in his fifties standing in the hallway leading in called out to them.

"Who're you?"

"I'm from Investigation Section One of the Metropolitan Police. We've come for Kiyomaru," Okumura answered.

"Ah…" The man's face scrunched in obvious displeasure.

A subsection chief of the prefectural police or thereabouts, Mekari guessed.

"Kiyomaru's currently receiving medical treatment, see. Could you folks wait back at South Station?"

Mekari approached him and asked, "Where is Kiyomaru now?"

"I just said he's receiving treatment."

"Yes, but where?"

"Didn't I just tell you he's in treatment?"

"I'm from the Security Section of the Metropolitan Police. I've been ordered to act as Kiyomaru's escort."

"Two of our young officers are with him, don't worry."

They weren't going to get anything from this man. Mekari left him and asked a passing nurse. She told him that the room was near the back on the first floor, at the corner on the left side.

Mekari quickly headed that way. Shiraiwa followed him.

"Who do you Tokyo Police think you are?" a curse, meant to be heard, resounded down the hall.

Because one of the Fukuoka South officers had attacked Kiyomaru, the prefectural police had lost face even as the entire nation watched. The Metropolitan Police was barging in almost as if on cue and demanding that the locals hand over Kiyomaru. Mekari understood why they might feel grumpy. Worse, telling them that the MPD would guard Kiyomaru made it sound like Fukuoka cops weren't up to it.

Despite all of that, Mekari had no intention of minding their feelings.

Since officers themselves were the most dangerous predators,

Kiyomaru had to be whisked away from Fukuoka Police.

The room they had been told to find was the ER.

Mekari quietly opened the door. The two plainclothes standing on the other side turned around.

Mekari and Shiraiwa entered.

"MPD Security Sec. We'll take over from here," Mekari informed them with no room for backtalk.

The two plainclothes weren't able to respond right away, and then Okumura and Kanbashi entered.

"You two, thanks for the hard work."

Okumura's words seemed to persuade the local detectives that they had no choice but to leave.

As they reluctantly stepped out of the treatment room, Okumura and Kanbashi walked straight to the back.

It appeared that Kiyomaru had already been treated, and a nurse was bandaging him up and down his left elbow.

It looked like the injury wasn't grave enough to hinder the transfer.

Seeing Kiyomaru in the flesh for the first time, Mekari felt a disconnect.

The man didn't look quite as vicious as in his photos. He also seemed far younger than thirty-four. His face had an intelligent cast, but also a lingering boyishness.

He didn't look like the perp of such brutal murders.

Was it because the current Kiyomaru was a victim who'd almost been killed? Maybe it was just that Mekari was seeing him that way now.

Okumura waited until the nurse finished wrapping the bandages before approaching. He presented his identification to the young physician.

"We're from the Tokyo Metropolitan Police. May I?"

When the doctor nodded, Okumura pulled a single piece of paper from the inner pocket of his suit and turned back to face Kiyomaru.

"Kunihide Kiyomaru, yes? You're under arrest on suspicion of murdering Chika Ninagawa. Here's the warrant." He spread it in front of Kiyomaru's face to show him.

Without looking up, Kiyomaru snorted.

When Kanbashi took out a pair of handcuffs, the doctor shook his head.

Okumura nodded, and Kanbashi put them away.

"6:02 p.m., routine arrest," Okumura murmured, looking at his watch.

With this, Kiyomaru was officially under the MPD's charge.

Going forward, Fukuoka Police would have to take orders from Tokyo Police and do their best to provide support.

Ordinarily, wanted suspects could be arrested by any department nationwide, but in this case, Fukuoka Police hadn't placed Kiyomaru under arrest. He had turned himself in, and technically, was being sheltered at a police station as the victim of an attempted murder.

This was because he needed to be presented to the prosecutor's office within forty-eight hours of his arrest. They had to buy as much time as possible for the transfer.

The customary practice, when a local headquarters was

entrusted with an arrest, was to request a "Type One Measure" whereby the local outfit also escorted the suspect. In this case, however, personnel from the special investigation headquarters had traveled to the station holding the suspect and executed the warrant upon meeting him.

"Even if you arrest me, I'll just end up getting killed," spat Kiyomaru.

"We won't let you get killed. As per the law, you'll be tried fair and square," Okumura said as if to correct him.

"Heh, as per law? Tryin' to act like the guardians of justice… I bet you're all thinkin' of killing me too. You want money that bad? Huh?!"

Kiyomaru's face flushed before their eyes, his expression a wild beast's.

Kanbashi brought his face close to the perp's and said, "Be a good boy or you'll just get hurt worse."

Kiyomaru stood up from his chair. "Stop trying to act cool and just kill me! Just try it! Take off one layer, and you're all just the same as me! Murderers!"

The doctor ordered the nurse to administer a sedative.

Okumura tapped Kanbashi's shoulder and made him back up.

"Those two guys over there are SPs with the MPD," he said. "They'll be protecting you during the transfer. You can relax."

Kiyomaru stared at Mekari and Shiraiwa with open hostility.

"Protect me?! Don't make me laugh. Get this, I won't trust anyone! The only one I can trust in this whole world is myself!"

Mekari couldn't care less. He was studying the nurse.

She looked oddly tense preparing the syringe.

Maybe it was only natural given that a brutal murderer of two little girls was screaming his head off, but for a veteran nurse who looked to be in her late thirties, her hands fidgeted a trifle too awkwardly as she sucked medicine into the syringe.

She snuck the small emptied bottle into the pocket of her scrubs.

Mekari moved.

Signaling Shiraiwa with his eyes, he stepped between the nurse and Kiyomaru.

With the syringe and a disinfectant wipe in hand, the nurse walked toward Kiyomaru but stopped. Mekari stood between them as though to hide Kiyomaru from her.

Mekari looked the nurse straight in the eye.

"What's inside the syringe?"

The nurse couldn't answer. She was frozen stiff.

"Please show me the container in your pocket."

The nurse was trembling. Even as she trembled, she fixed Mekari with a terrible glare.

Shiraiwa had already pulled out his SIG. He had it steadied with both hands and with the barrel pointed to the floor.

Kanbashi rushed over and snatched the syringe from the nurse's hand. The doctor grabbed the small bottle out of the nurse's pocket and looked at the label.

"KCl..."

"What kind of medicine is that?" Kanbashi asked the speech-less doctor.

"It's potassium chloride. It's a drug we use often every day.

But…"

"But what?"

"We usually administer it via a drip, and never IV it."

"IV?"

"Oh, an intravenous injection."

"What happens when it's injected directly?" Mekari asked.

"Um, with a rapid intravenous injection, it would cause hyperkalemia…"

Mekari waited for the doctor's next words.

"You'd go into cardiac arrest…"

As though all the strength had left her body, the nurse crumpled to the floor.

Okumura watched her with sad eyes.

Kiyomaru's face was sheet white, as though he were already a corpse.

The nurse who had tried to kill Kiyomaru was arrested by investigators from Fukuoka Police and taken to South Station. For the moment, Kiyomaru had been moved to an empty hospital room and shot with sedative under Mekari's watchful eyes.

As soon as the effects kicked in, Kiyomaru fell asleep. He'd no doubt barely gotten any sleep since the night before.

Mekari and Shiraiwa brought folding chairs into the hallway and sat outside Kiyomaru's room. Surely the most effective way to protect Kiyomaru was to keep everyone away from him.

Once the transfer got going, however, things wouldn't be that easy.

Already in the last twenty-four hours, Kiyomaru had nearly

been killed three times.

The man who'd sheltered him. A policeman. A female nurse.

Anyone could become a murderer in this unique situation, given the opportunity.

It was Mekari's job to crush such opportunities before they arose.

But it all depended on the method of transfer, which had been planned out by the National Police Agency's Security Division.

Okumura and Kanbashi, who'd gone to the prefectural police headquarters to ascertain that method, brought someone back with them. Okumura introduced him to Mekari and Shiraiwa.

Sergeant Kenji Sekiya, Investigation Section One, Fukuoka Prefectural Police. He was the final member of the transfer team.

A sturdily built man in his early forties, both his eyebrows and neck were thick. He would have passed as the former captain of Kobe Steel's indomitable rugby squad.

After Mekari and Shiraiwa exchanged greetings with the sergeant, Okumura said with a grim expression, "We've got a bit of a problem."

A left-wing extremist group was threatening to do the deed. Following the Minister of Justice's press conference, it had sent out a statement to various media: "In order to wipe the state apparatus clean of authority, we will kill Kunihide Kiyomaru using every means available to us."

Public Security—which dealt with hardcore political cadres—was still investigating the authenticity of the statement, but there was no time. Taking the threat seriously, the National Police Agency had ordered thorough defenses.

Apparently the man on the case from NPA headquarters had already come to Fukuoka.

All airline companies had announced their refusal to let Kiyomaru board. Their rationale was that if something happened, they couldn't guarantee the safety of the other passengers.

In addition, word from Public Security was that a combined total of about a dozen SA-7 hand-held surface-to-air missile launchers and RPG-7 anti-tank rocket launchers from the former Soviet military had been brought within national borders.

Most of the weapons were assumed to be in the hands of left-wing guerillas. Helicopters and ships would be choice targets for acts of terrorism.

To be honest, Mekari didn't want to ride in a chopper with Kiyomaru. In Iraq, even Black Hawks, the American attack helicopters, had been shot down multiple times. He didn't think they could escape a missile that detected an engine's infra-red rays and clung to them.

On a ship too, if the whole vessel sank there wasn't much Mekari could do.

After due consideration, the National Police Agency had decided on using highways to conduct the transfer with a battalion of riot police—three hundred and fifty men.

They were departing tomorrow morning at seven.

Riot police from local and adjacent prefectures would line the route, with a total of sixteen thousand personnel mobilized.

Using a sea of riot police was the National Police Agency's specialty.

It seemed that they would be able to stop all attacks from

without. But traveling from Fukuoka to Tokyo by car surrounded by three hundred and fifty riot police armed with guns worried Mekari to no end.

At that moment, the man he'd had a disagreement with upon arriving at the hospital appeared.

According to Sekiya, and exactly as Mekari had thought, he was a subsection chief from the prefectural police's investigation section.

"We're going to move Kiyomaru back to South Station. You guys can leave now."

Mekari stepped forward. "We will be the ones guarding Kiyomaru."

"Your job is to guard him during the transfer. Are we transferring right now? Well?!"

He sounded grossly triumphant.

"While you're here, leave it to the people here!"

It appeared nothing could get through to this man.

Tapping Mekari's shoulder, Sekiya whispered in his ear, "Maybe let the old man have a bit of the spotlight too? I'll take responsibility…"

In that case, Mekari didn't mind. It wasn't like he actually cared about Kiyomaru's well-being.

If only he got murdered tonight… we'd be able to fly home tomorrow by plane.

Chapter 2

Three Hundred Fifty People

1

His wife was alive.

When he arrived home the layout of the rooms had changed, and the one room was awfully large. Sitting up on a bed at the back of the large room, his wife looked his way and smiled.

Hadn't she died?

The next moment, he understood everything.

Right, I'd come home somehow having convinced myself that my wife was dead.

So, after continued treatment, at last she'd been discharged from the hospital today.

What a bummer, if she'd told him he'd have gone to pick her up.

His wife continued to smile and to stare at him silently.

I'm laughing, he thought. Laughing and crying so hard the back of his nose felt numb.

Pure happiness welled up from the bottom of his heart and soaked all the way to his fingertips.

The tears that rolled down his cheek and into his mouth tasted salty.

Even so, he continued to laugh. He ran to his wife, still

laughing, and hugged her tight.

His wife heartily returned his embrace.

She was thin, but it was unmistakably his wife's body. Her warmth felt so nostalgic.

How stupid I've been.

To have thought her dead, and to have suffered through so much sorrow.

Because he was still embracing his wife, he couldn't see her face, but he felt her fingertips on his back.

Why wasn't she saying anything?

The moment he entertained that thought, his wife finally whispered into his ear.

"Thank you, and sorry…"

That was when Mekari woke up. He was on the bed in the hotel they were staying at.

He recognized his wife's smile as the one in her portrait on the altar. No wonder it hadn't moved.

He wondered how many times he'd had such dreams. And like every other time he'd awoken from them, Mekari wanted nothing more than to die.

It was a bit past three in the morning. There was still some time to go back to sleep, but he didn't feel he could.

He got up and removed a pack of cigarettes and a lighter from his small travel bag. The cigarettes were Seven Stars, the same brand he'd been buying since college. He sat back down on the bed and lit one.

Mekari had quit smoking when he'd been appointed an SP.

SPs had to operate according to the schedule of the VIP under guard. Going without food or a bathroom break for long periods of time was part of the job description. Needless to say, a smoking habit didn't help.

Yet ever since he'd learned of his wife's illness, he'd been unable to let cigarettes out of sight.

These days he almost never actually lighted up, but he carried them around for when he felt the desperate need for a smoke.

Like now.

Mekari wanted to die.

Ever since his wife's passing, he'd wanted to. He found no joy in living.

But he couldn't die.

Because his wife was always watching.

He couldn't die because he knew his wife didn't wish it. Because if she learned that he was a weak man who'd chosen death, unable to bear the sorrow, she'd feel let down.

He couldn't die when he remembered how guilty his wife would feel.

It had been a while since nicotine had flooded his body. His consciousness effortlessly drifted away. It was a bit like the moment before he passed out caught in a judo strangle hold.

His hands and feet were cooling.

He could clearly feel his heartbeat.

He felt like he was experiencing the comforts and discomforts of smoking all at the same time.

Maybe he felt such a craving for cigarettes when he was really down because smoking let him picture himself gently gliding toward death.

That could be it.

The transfer would begin in a few hours.

Since no one had contacted them, Mekari assumed Kiyomaru was still alive. It looked like they wouldn't be able to fly back after all.

The original plan had been for their team of five to transfer Kiyomaru, with guidance from the National Police Agency and support from prefectural police along the way.

But the left-wing extremists' statement forced them to alter their plan substantially.

They were shifting from "a concealed transfer" and avoiding the public gaze to "an intimidating transfer" that would display overwhelming armed force.

Mekari thought the change may have been due to more than just preparing for left-wing guerillas. Perhaps they hoped to avert the eyes of the media away from "an officer assaulting Kiyomaru," a fact that greatly dented trust in the police, and to make "the threat of terrorism" the immediate focus. In that sense, the extremists' statement served the brass all too well.

The timing just seemed very convenient. Was it perhaps an act put on by the police?

Mekari was almost ready to believe it.

Either way, none of that mattered. The upshot was that he

was heading out to do a miserable job in a miserable mood.

Mekari considered going out and getting something to eat, but he had no appetite. He took a shower, but his mood didn't improve in the slightest.

He turned on the television. The early morning news was reporting from in front of Fukuoka South Station. It was so early that there weren't many spectators yet, but that only served to emphasize the number of press people.

In response to questioning, the officer who'd attacked Kiyomaru supposedly confessed, "I didn't know there was a bounty on Kiyomaru. I just couldn't forgive his crimes. I wasn't trying to kill him."

It sounded so incredibly fake. At the same time, it would probably be difficult to prove that he was lying.

The news said the questioning of the female nurse would commence in earnest starting in the afternoon.

The screen cut back to the studio and moved on to the transfer that would begin at 7 a.m. They said they were putting together a special news program to broadcast it live. Every channel was most likely doing the same.

Apparently the Kiyomaru Site had already posted in detail the convoy's makeup, route, and ETAs for specific locations. A journalist commentator speculated, "Perhaps they have an insider within the force?"

Despite the police's frantic efforts to shut down the Kiyomaru Site, it was based overseas. They were facing difficulties and planned to send investigators to the country soon.

Taking the attacks by a detainment officer and by a medical professional very seriously, the government had issued a comment: "Our policy is to severely punish anyone who is manipulated by the foolish bounty into killing the suspect. We are also considering reforming the law on lifetime imprisonment."

This was nothing more than a bluff by the government, Mekari thought. If they were considering changing the law now, how long would it take for the bill to pass through the Diet?

The climax of the show was today. He couldn't help but think it was all pointless.

The phone next to the bed rang. It was Shiraiwa.

After telling him to meet in the lobby at five, Mekari put down the receiver and began to change.

He put on a bulletproof vest over a white t-shirt. Ever since they'd switched to a high-tech material called "Spectra," the vests had become exceptionally thin and light, unnoticeable even under a collared shirt. Anti-ballistic performance had also improved enough to stop even a .44 magnum shot fired at point-blank range. Even the high-penetration Tokarev AP bullets which could rip through the Kevlar vests used until the earlier nineties would be unable to pierce the Spectra Shield (Type III-A) that Mekari now wore. It was even said to prevent most injuries, such as to the ribs, that went with taking a bullet.

But Mekari had never been shot before. He didn't know how much damage he'd actually suffer.

He finished buttoning his white collared shirt and tightened a drab-colored tie around his neck.

To the front of the right side of his belt, he attached the Bianchi-brand Inside Pants Holster that housed the SIG P228. Hanging from the belt by a clip, and specifically designed for concealment, the holster hid the gun along with itself on the inner side of the pants. The pouch holding two extra magazines for the SIG he attached to the left side of his belt.

The MPD threefold baton, a frosted black special affair, went on the right side or back of the belt in a designated case.

He put on a navy suit jacket. SPs never buttoned their outerwear during missions. They needed to draw quickly.

Mekari checked himself in the mirror. It didn't look like he was armed with a large caliber pistol and forty rounds of bullets.

Shiraiwa had their other equipment, but whether they'd come into use remained to be seen.

The hotel had agreed to send to the Metropolitan Police all four of their travel bags, containing their change of clothes.

After debating for a moment, Mekari put the cigarettes and lighter in the pocket of his jacket.

Mekari and the other three arrived at South Station at exactly six. They had already finished eating breakfast at a diner close to the hotel. He hadn't had any appetite, but he needed to eat when he had the chance.

The area around the station was overflowing with reporters and onlookers.

Close to a dozen news helicopters flew overhead, and the intense whirring of their blades heightened the imposing mood.

When the MPD cops entered the small conference room on

the second floor, Sekiya was there waiting for them.

He gave them cheerful greetings. He looked tough but was a rather pleasant man.

Before long, Kiyomaru was brought in by four detainment officers. He had probably been assigned four so they could police each other.

After they left, it was decided that Kiyomaru would wear a bulletproof vest.

He could still barely move his left arm. They took off his hooded gray sweater, and the vest was slipped over his head and secured with velcro by Shiraiwa.

Kiyomaru was obedient. Although some color had returned to his face since yesterday, his eyes were dark.

Shiraiwa headed to the parking lot ahead of the others to check the transport vehicle.

At five minutes before seven, they were told that everything was in place.

The team minus Shiraiwa huddled around Kiyomaru as they left the conference room.

When they reached the service exit facing the parking lot at the back of South Station, they saw that a hunkering blue bus with a white line running down its side had been pulled up. It was the riot police's large-type transport.

All of the windows were covered in metal wiring.

It was capable of holding one platoon of thirty-five riot police, but apart from the driver, only Kiyomaru and the five transfer team members would board.

They seated Kiyomaru on the right side around midway down the bus. Shiraiwa sat in front of him, and Mekari sat beside him on the left side. Okumura and Kanbashi sat behind Mekari, and Sekiya sat behind Kiyomaru.

It hit seven. A whistle sounded somewhere.

The engines of the many vehicles waiting in the parking lot rumbled. The procession began to move.

Large-type transports packed with riot police passed before them one after the other. Then finally, the bus with Mekari's team set out.

2

The transfer force left South Station and went south down regular streets, entering Fukuoka City Highway 5 from Itazuke.

They were a massive procession of twenty vehicles. A roving unit was at the front, acting as scouts. Following at a considerable distance from one another in case emergency evasive measures became necessary were, in order: two guiding patrol cars from the prefectural highway police, four large-type transports holding a platoon of riot police each, the battalion command car, the protected vehicle that Mekari and the others were on, the security command car, an additional five large-type transports, a large ambulance for the worst-case scenario, the rear roving unit, and a patrol car from the highway squad.

The three hundred and fifty riot police assigned as guards were not Fukuoka Police, but rather from the Kyushu District

Division. It gathered personnel from each prefecture in the district. Both of Fukuoka Riot Police's two units were protecting the route, and apparently, neighboring Oita prefecture's riot police had been dispatched to assist.

The transfer force would pass through City Highway 2 and get on the Kyushu Expressway from Dazaifu IC. Once in Shimonoseki past the Kanmon Straits, Yamaguchi prefectural police and Chugoku Division riot police would take over.

After that, the baton would pass in turn to the prefectural polices of Hiroshima, Okayama, Hyogo, Osaka, Kyoto, Shiga, Aichi, and Shizuoka, and finally the MPD. The riot police division in charge would switch to Kinki's in Hyogo prefecture, Chubu's in Aichi prefecture, and Kanto's in Kanagawa prefecture. The only vehicles that would run the length of the entire trip would be the protected vehicle holding Kiyomaru and the security command car carrying the men in charge from the National Police Agency.

The highways traveled by the transfer force would be blocked section by section, preventing civilian vehicles from entering.

They would shut down the outbound lane on City Highway 2, and the inbound lanes—which headed toward the capital—from the Kyushu Expressway onwards. As they passed, the blockade behind them would be removed as a new one was placed ahead.

The transfer force was making good headway, but the inbound lane of City Highway 2 was congested. It was what you might call a sight-seeing jam. All of the drivers were driving slowly and gawking at the fearsome column that was the transfer force.

Outside the wire-shielded windows, the skies were mostly cloudy.

Almost as though they were reflecting Mekari's mood.

The whirring of the helicopter rotors had been bothersome at first, but he was used to it now. Being broadcast live nationwide by those choppers, however, didn't feel real. A fearsome number of eyes had to be glued to TV screens.

Mekari wondered what was so interesting about it. The only explanation was that they were eagerly awaiting some kind of attack.

"This is seriously just a waste of tax money…" Kanbashi broke the silence. "Scum like this, we should just stuff in a steel box and send as freight cargo."

Mekari agreed that it was a bit extreme. No doubt everyone on the transfer team thought the same. They weren't even needed anymore.

"Hey! You laughed just now, didn't you?!" Kanbashi raised his voice.

"Not really…" Kiyomaru answered with a hint of a sneer.

"Did I say something amusing? Did I say anything that would make you laugh at me?" Kanbashi pressed.

He was probably bored. It seemed like he was trying to pick on Kiyomaru.

"Yesterday you'd almost been killed and looked as pale as a corpse, but you're awfully cocky today."

Kiyomaru didn't respond and instead kept gazing through the window.

"Hey, you ignoring me? Hey, hey you, freak. Face this way." Kanbashi was being pretty persistent. "Hey, pervert. Is sex with an elementary school girl really that good?"

"Tut, let's stop it there," Sekiya cut in.

If he hadn't, Mekari would have.

Kanbashi's needling was unpleasant. Mekari didn't want to hear Kiyomaru's answer, either.

"Nothing'll come of you bullying Kiyomaru now," Sekiya said.

Kanbashi turned to him, making no effort to conceal his annoyance. "You and the SP guys will be done once we reach Tokyo, but we have to deal with this freak for some time to come. I figured we should start getting to know each other."

"Is this an interrogation room? It's a fact that people are after Kiyomaru's life. If you want to get friendly with him, why not start by easing his fears?" chided Sekiya.

"Ease his fears? Wow, you're awfully nice to this perverted piece of murdering scum," Kanbashi shot back sarcastically. "Trash like him should be living in fear of death."

"You want me to die, right?" Kiyomaru turned around to face Kanbashi. "You think I should just die, don't you?"

"Huh?" Kanbashi froze at the sudden question.

"You can't answer? I asked you if you want me to die."

"Yeah, of course. The world's better without scum like you!"

"Then kill me."

"What?"

"If it'll make the world a better place, why don't you just kill me? You'll even get a billion yen."

"Way to talk, you bastard…"

"What? You can't kill me? There's a freak you want dead right here, it'll better the world, and you'll get a ton of money, but you lack the courage to become a murderer? Is that it?"

Mekari thought that Kanbashi might lunge at Kiyomaru, but he didn't. "Don't push it or one of us five might start wanting that one billion," Kanbashi said.

Kiyomaru snorted. "He can't kill me himself, so he passes it on to his friends."

"You fucker, you better watch yourself."

Kiyomaru just calmly looked back at Kanbashi. "You got kids?"

"Huh?"

"At that age, you're married, right? You have any kids?"

Kanbashi's face flushed. "What's that got to do with anything!"

"I thought so… You were awfully eager to pick on me, and it's 'cause you've got a kid the same age as the victims. Feels kinda personal, huh?"

Kanbashi had been trying to rile up Kiyomaru but was getting cornered instead.

"Is it a girl? Oh, she is. Ha ha ha…"

"Enough!" Sekiya snapped and shouted.

But Kiyomaru ignored him. "How about I answer your question, then. I could give you all the details on how good sex with an elementary school girl is."

He was laughing. He was enjoying this.

"I told you to shut up!" Sekiya bellowed, reaching over from behind and grabbing Kiyomaru's collar.

Kiyomaru just continued to laugh and drew his face closer to Kanbashi's to say, "You're curious, right? I bet you're dying to know what it'd be like to stick it in your own daughter."

Kanbashi stood up. "You want me to make it so you can never laugh again?" His own taut expression resembled a grin.

Mekari had stood up at almost the same time. He got in between them and faced Kanbashi.

"I won't kill him," Kanbashi promised and tried to shove Mekari to the side.

Mekari slapped his hand away.

"You can't strike him even if it's not to kill him."

"You're taking his side?" Kanbashi turned his rage on Mekari.

"My job is to protect Kiyomaru," Mekari answered calmly.

"You heard what he just said, didn't you?! I can't let him get away with that!"

"I can't let you put one finger on Kiyomaru. There's no guarantee that you're not after the one billion."

"Say that again, you bastard!"

Kanbashi looked to be on the verge of exploding.

"Mekari."

Okumura, who'd been watching their exchange expressionlessly, finally spoke. "Is this your first time interacting with a murder convict?"

"Well, yes, what of it?"

Mekari didn't have any experience with violent criminals. After serving at a police box in a precinct's community section, and starting with a stint with the riot police, his career path was mostly security-oriented.

"There are two types of murderers. Fools for whom you ought to feel sympathy, and human scum. This man's typical scum."

Mekari already knew that. Everyone in Japan knew that Kiyomaru was nothing but filth.

"What Kiyomaru said just now was degrading to the victim. No investigator of violent crimes would let that go."

"I see. However, being from Security Sec, I can't agree. If you want to rough up Kiyomaru, please do so in the interrogation room once we've arrived at headquarters. Then, it'll have nothing to do with me."

Saying his due, Mekari returned to his seat next to Kiyomaru and sat down.

Silence reigned in the vehicle again.

Kiyomaru gazed through the wire mesh window as though nothing had happened.

The Kyushu Expressway's outbound lanes—headed away from Tokyo—were horrendously congested. Rows of stopped cars continued on endlessly.

Mekari didn't know how bad it usually got at this hour, but there was no mistaking that the traffic jam was caused by a large turnout of spectators.

He was aware that perhaps not all of them were just rubbernecking. Someone aiming to attack Kiyomaru might be concealed in their midst. But he didn't think it would be possible to mount an effective assault. If someone fired a gun, the transfer force would immediately speed past.

In fact, without, say, the anti-tank missiles that Public Security had warned about, it seemed that the convoy could hardly be slowed down. Even if such a weapon were in play, it would be difficult to ascertain which of the ten identical vehicles carried Kiyomaru. Wreaking havoc on the riot police was an option, but killing Kiyomaru seemed like a daunting task.

If the NPA took the threat of missile and rocket assaults seriously, Mekari thought, they'd have blockaded the outbound lane as well.

"Mr. Mekari, check this out..." Shiraiwa turned around in the seat in front and offered Mekari his cell phone. "I was looking at the mobile Kiyomaru Site and..."

The screen showed a detailed map. Every vehicle in the convoy on the Kyushu Expressway was discernible as a dot.

Among the twenty or so black dots was a single red one. It marked the position of the bus that Mekari and the others, along with Kiyomaru, were on.

He was stunned.

The accurate tracking of the transfer force itself was no surprise. It was being broadcast live on television. Everyone knew.

But how had they pinpointed Kiyomaru's position?

The info hadn't been shared with the media, naturally. Kiyomaru had been put on one of many transports in order to create uncertainty. Was it such an easy guess for experts? Was insider information really getting leaked?

In any case, the map was disturbingly precise. Car navigation systems had nothing on it.

Mekari recalled footage from a U.S. military satellite he'd once seen on the news. The website had to be abusing a system originally developed for military purposes.

When he zoomed out on the display, it switched to a wide-scope map. A single red dot was slowly moving east on the Kyu-shu Expressway near the city of Nogata.

Suddenly, a voice rang from the bus's wireless speaker.

"All vehicles, emergency stop!"

Mekari placed his hand on the gun at his waist.

3

They had no idea what was going on. Mekari and the others held their breath in the halted large transport.

They could hear intermittent exchanges over the wireless in-tercom but still didn't have a clue. There was no mistaking that something unexpected had happened, but it didn't appear as though the situation required Mekari to pull out his gun.

Okumura and Kanbashi headed to the security command car for an explanation. They could have asked over the wireless intercom—but probably wanted to keep Kiyomaru in the dark as much as possible.

Kiyomaru didn't seem afraid. Mekari didn't feel particularly tense, either.

Halting the transfer force meant something had happened in the front. Had someone broken through the blockade? Even then, it probably wouldn't affect Mekari or Kiyomaru in any se-rious way.

Mekari was more worried about the outbound lanes. With the transfer force sitting tight, the congestion had turned into a standstill, and more and more people were getting out of their cars.

There was a crowd forming at the divider. From just what Mekari could see, several hundred people were standing out on the road.

A loud external announcement boomed, requesting civilians to return to their cars immediately. It continued that armed force would be employed if the instructions weren't followed with due haste—the riot police's bread-and-butter line.

But no one moved to obey. The swarm of people only grew in thickness and length.

What if they turned into a violent mob? What if they climbed over the divider and surrounded the convoy? How would three hundred and fifty riot police deal with the few thousand that the crowd had swelled to become?

Even if the crowd rioted, it was hard to imagine being ordered to fire at civilians.

Most likely, tear gas would be used to suppress them, but it easily dispersed in open air, and there was a limit to the number of shots. Riot police reinforcements would probably arrive one after the other, but the crowd, too, could multiply endlessly.

It was still doubtful that Kiyomaru would come to any harm, but they'd be trapped in the vehicle and rendered immobile. Continuing the transfer would become impossible. They couldn't block the outbound side at this point though, when it was already so congested.

It appeared that the transfer force had no choice but to keep moving without hesitation.

Mekari realized that he still had Shiraiwa's cell phone in his left hand.

The red dot on the map was static.

He called out to Shiraiwa and returned the phone. Shiraiwa seemed to have forgotten too, distracted by the outbound lanes.

The phone was new. Mekari didn't know if it was cutting edge, but it certainly was in design.

Mekari's own cell phone was old. He believed it was even the first generation of models that used the i-mode mobile internet service. Compared to Shiraiwa's phone, its screen was small and its display grainy.

Yet Mekari had no intention of buying a new one. It wasn't just that his wife had chosen it for him. If he switched to a new model, all of his saved text messages would be lost.

Mekari didn't text. In his whole life, he'd never exchanged them except with his wife.

The messages from his wife were his treasure, and at the same time, a chronicle of sorrow.

Thanks to his transfer to the mobile security contingent, Mekari could visit his wife every day after she was hospitalized. Still, he wasn't able to stay by her side around the clock.

The hours he spent together with her were but a small part of his day. At other times, all he had to look forward to were the texts she sent him in secret from the nurse.

Around once a week, Mekari brought his wife's cell phone home to recharge it. It was something he could do for her, as meager as it was.

His wife also enjoyed receiving his texts. She sent back

messages several times the length of his succinct ones.

Mekari gradually got used to it and was able to text her things he couldn't tell her in person. Mostly, he seemed to recall, words of gratitude.

He thought their love deepened as their parting drew near.

At one point, he sent his first text that said, "I love you."

He naturally expected the reply to be "I love you, too." But the words that came back were "Thank you, and sorry."

It had been heartbreaking, the last text from his wife.

Okumura and Kanbashi finally returned.

According to Okumura's rundown, a vehicle really had broken through the blockade.

Several kilometers ahead of them at the barrier on the Hachiman exit, a large semi-trailer had driven down the inbound side and tried to approach them from the front. A security police car was dispatched immediately to pursue it, and the wireless intercom message had been transmitted at that time.

From the transfer force, the roving unit in the vanguard and the highway police's guiding car reacted quickly by parking sideways to block the lanes.

The sandwiched semi-trailer, recklessly trying to break through, rammed headlong into the vehicles. The police car sustained heavy damage, but the trailer crashed into the sidewall and stopped.

All personnel had distanced themselves and none were injured.

The only person on the trailer, the driver, was arrested on the spot.

They were currently cleaning up the aftermath to make way for the transfer force, and it would take a while longer until they could move.

It wasn't a very well thought-out attack. The likelihood of it having succeeded was almost zero.

It seemed to Mekari as though people had caught a virus spread by Ninagawa called "a billion yen" and lost their common sense. Were such pointless attacks in store all along the way? There was no knowing when they'd actually make it to Tokyo, then.

Moreover, according to what Okumura had learned, on the outbound side of their route, which comprised the Kyushu, Kanmon, Chugoku, Meishin, and Tomei Expressways, traffic congestion reached all the way to the Kansai region.

Frequent quarrels were erupting between drivers frustrated at the total standstill, one case even escalating to murder. Forty-odd other cases had resulted in injury.

It was as though the entire country was trapped in a feverish daze.

Perhaps they'd chosen the wrong transfer method after all. Dangling a raw fish in hand, they were hoping to walk past a posse of starving stray cats. The fish might not get stolen, but it was a given that they'd be set upon by feline after feline. And what if a wolf saw an opening and snuck up on them?

A top-secret transfer that concealed Kiyomaru's presence seemed like the only way to go. With the current method, Mekari feared that their problems wouldn't be limited to the outbound lanes.

Although they were only blockading parts of the inbound side at a time, they'd thrown the nation's distribution system into chaos—probably far more than the planners had anticipated, just as the outbound congestion far exceeded expectations. The traffic diverted from expressways would be forced onto regular roads, which were fated to see major congestion, too.

How long more could they keep up this transfer method? If another incident occurred, they would no doubt be pressed to change tactics. Perhaps the National Police Agency brass were already reconsidering other options.

"Hey, you…"

It was Kiyomaru's voice. Mekari turned around to face him.

"Are you serious about protecting me?" Kiyomaru said in a whisper that only Mekari could hear.

"That's my duty."

"I know that. Given your duty, I'm asking if you're serious about protecting me."

"I'll do everything I can to follow through."

"Hah, 'everything I can'…"

Kiyomaru snorted and turned back to face out through the window.

What was the guy trying to say?

It might not have been anything. But he'd cast a small ripple in Mekari's mind.

Was he serious about protecting Kiyomaru?

He certainly didn't intend on slacking. His pride as an SP wouldn't allow that.

But am I serious about protecting Kiyomaru?

After resuming the transfer, the convoy made good headway and entered the Kanmon Expressway.

They would soon leave Kyushu.

The last parking area on Japan's southernmost major island was called the Mekari PA. It was the first time Mekari had heard of a place that shared his name. However, since the writing was phonetic, he didn't know what characters it used.

A sign that read "Mekari Park" sped by. Although spelled out in characters this time, they differed from the ones in his surname, and he wasn't even sure if you read it that way.

Once they passed Mekari PA, the Kanmon Bridge came into view ahead of them. By crossing it they would enter Shimonoseki City in Yamaguchi, the westernmost prefecture on Honshu, Japan's main island.

At Dan-no-Ura PA, on the edge of Shimonoseki, the Yamaguchi Police and the Chugoku Riot Police Division would take over.

The transfer force began crossing the Kanmon Bridge.

The wind was strong up here. Mekari could feel the giant suspension bridge subtly swaying.

The outbound lanes were still just as congested.

Mekari had learned for the first time that the famous Dan-no-Ura, the site of the final battle between the Genji and the Heike, was located in Shimonoseki.

The opposite shore was Dan-no-Ura. The Heike, or Taira clan, had been annihilated there. "Dan-no-Ura" had a melancholic ring to it.

Mekari felt as though he'd caught the scent of death.

The Yamaguchi Police and the Chugoku Riot Police were on standby at Dan-no-Ura PA. Close to a dozen helicopters still hovered overhead.

The moment the transfer force halted, people started scrambling about. Once the swap was complete, the new convoy would move out.

Suddenly, someone knocked on the door of the large transport Mekari and the others were on.

The police officer serving as their driver opened the door. Shiraiwa quickly stood up and headed to it.

The person who entered was a member of the riot police.

"I have a message from Senior Superintendent Takamine."

Apart from lacking the special acrylic tower shield, the guy was fully equipped. He wore a helmet, and an armored vest over his regulation uniform. Armguards made out of special polycarbonate resin and covered in black vinyl leather protected the area from his elbows to the back of his hands.

However, the special acrylic face mask on his helmet was fully lowered, which Mekari found odd.

He stood up and stepped into the aisle.

"Is Assistant Inspector Okumura from the Metropolitan Police present?"

At the riot policeman's question, Shiraiwa turned towards Okumura, and as soon as he did, the intruder shoved him to the side and charged towards Kiyomaru. His right hand pulled out a New Nambu revolver.

When the muzzle pointed towards Kiyomaru, Mekari reflexively dove in front of the gun.

Two orange lights flashed before his eyes.

As the stunning reports rang out, all sound vanished.

Mekari saw what looked like dust dance off of his body.

4

He couldn't breathe.

And he couldn't hear anything.

Shiraiwa grabbed the riot policeman by the collar and yanked him down to the floor.

Flames ran from the New Nambu's muzzle to the ceiling.

Shiraiwa had a terrifying expression as he pressed the barrel of his SIG into the intruder's throat and yelled something. Pinned down in the aisle, his opponent dropped his New Nambu and raised both hands.

The fact that Mekari could see meant he was also lying in the aisle.

Someone propped him upright from behind.

"Hey, hang in there!"

Sekiya's voice sounded faint and distant.

The riot policeman who had assaulted Kiyomaru was put in handcuffs by Kanbashi and handed over to Yamaguchi Police.

Two of the .38 Special ammo fired from the New Nambu revolver had been stopped by Mekari's vest.

His ribs had been spared any damage whatsoever.

Still, the impact of bullets at point-blank range had been tremendous. Mekari had literally been blown off his feet.

Maybe that was what a punch to the chest from a pro heavyweight boxer felt like, too.

But even more fearsome had been the reports. The sound of gunfire in the vehicle's enclosed space was, in a word, stunning.

Mekari felt intense pain in his ear. He was positive that the shockwaves had been enough to rupture his eardrums. He could even feel blood trickling from his ear holes.

In reality, there was no blood and his eardrums hadn't been ruptured, but it took a while for his hearing to return.

The greatest damage, however, persisted in Mekari's heart and mind.

He was shocked that he'd reflexively acted as Kiyomaru's shield.

Although he came out unscathed thanks to his bulletproof vest, if even one of the bullets had strayed a little higher, he would have died instantly. The vest only covered the torso. If you were shot in the neck or higher, without extraordinary luck, you were a goner.

Mekari had never felt death so close.

Didn't I want to die? Finding no joy in life, wasn't I hoping to bite it so I could go see my wife already?

Yet, his heart refused—refused to die as Kiyomaru's shield.

Mekari didn't wish death on Kiyomaru. At least, not now. But the fellow couldn't complain if he did get killed.

He'd robbed two innocent girls of their lives. For his own

goddamn pleasure.

Why should Mekari put his life on the line to protect a man like Kiyomaru?

Because it was his job? Because he was a member of the police organization?

Mekari had no reason to go that far and stay a cop.

If he died protecting someone not worth protecting, what meaning would his death have? Would it contribute to society in some way?

What would his wife think of him if he died like that?

I can't die for Kiyomaru.

Mekari was now clear on that point.

It was around twenty minutes after Kiyomaru had been assaulted by a riot policeman that the NPA honchos came over from the security command vehicle and boarded their large transport.

Mekari could now hear normally, although pain remained in his ears.

The three men who arrived were Senior Superintendent Takamine, Security Section Deputy Chief, NPA Security Division; Superintendent Yamanaka, from Public Security Section Three; and Superintendent Ishii, Highway Management Officer, Chugoku Police Division.

"Which one of you is Assistant Inspector Mekari?"

Senior Superintendent Takamine looked around forty, had a prominent forehead, and sported silver-rimmed glasses, the very picture of an elite.

"That would be me, sir," Mekari answered, standing up.

"How is your body holding up?"

"I'm good to go."

"I'm glad that in the end, there weren't any injuries." As thanks went, this was awfully impersonal. "We're fully aware of our responsibility. I've got to say, someone from the riot police assigned as security harboring such an inexcusable idea was an unfortunate accident, but as the one in charge here, I'd like to apologize to all of you regardless."

Though he said this, Takamine didn't bow his head, not even a fraction.

His empty words skimmed over Mekari's ears.

Despite his stated intent, Takamine actually looked proud to be delivering his speech. He seemed ready to enter the political world in the near future.

"After reassessing the situation, we've concluded that we can no longer continue the transfer via our current method."

Sensing that Takamine's speech would be long-winded, Mekari took a seat.

"You mean we can't allow any more riot troops to assault Kiyomaru?" Okumura cut through the act.

"Our main concern isn't Kiyomaru's life," Takamine stated without missing a beat. "The situation that will arise if Kiyomaru gets killed is the problem."

Mekari looked at Kiyomaru, who was looking out the window. His expression didn't change at all.

"It follows that Kiyomaru getting killed by our own people will reflect worst, not just on the force, but on our nation."

"So we'd rather have him killed by a civilian?" Kanbashi cut in. "In that case, we're all set if Kiyomaru just kills himself."

Takamine seemed to be the type who never dreamed that people might level sarcasm at him. He continued, "Well, that would wrap things up nicely with the least expenditure of the people's precious tax dollars, I don't deny it," he said with a faint smile.

What was Kiyomaru feeling at this man's words? Mekari couldn't read anything from the suspect's expression.

"So how do you intend to alter the transfer method going forward?" Okumura pressed Takamine for his conclusion.

"No, we're canceling for today."

"What?!" Shiraiwa let out a shocked shout.

"We'll go to the prefectural PD and, consulting Agency headquarters as well, we'll start hammering out a new transfer scheme."

Okumura stood up. "Then, the five of us will continue to transfer Kiyomaru on our own."

This time, it was Superintendent Yamanaka who blurted out, "What?"

Takamine gazed at Okumura mockingly.

"You seriously believe we'd let the likes…let your small team handle a situation of this magnitude?"

Had he wanted to say *the likes of you grunts*?

Okumura didn't show a speck of uncertainty. "We're acting under orders from the MPD's Head Criminal Investigator. If it's to transfer the suspect we'll follow the NPA's instructions, but if not, we'll simply proceed relying on ourselves. Our job is to transfer Kiyomaru to the MPD without delay and to present him before a prosecutor. We don't have the time to be discussing public affairs, unlike you people."

The trio from the National Police Agency were at a loss for words.

Okumura said to Kanbashi, "Hey, go tell the Yamaguchi Police whatever and borrow two patrol cars. Make sure they come with drivers who know the area."

"Got it!"

Kanbashi started off, a grin on his face, and tried to slip past Takamine and the others.

"Wait," yelled the senior superintendent, grabbing his shoulder, "you're not doing anything without my permission!"

Kanbashi pointed at Okumura with his chin. "I'm that guy's bitch, not yours. If you've got any complaints, send them to the Metropolitan Police."

Shaking off Takamine's hand, Kanbashi dashed out of the bus.

The sudden turn of events put Sekiya, the only man on the team from Fukuoka Police, in a delicate position, but he seemed completely charmed by Okumura's bravado.

"I'm sure the National Police Agency has its reasons, but would it be possible for you to leave Kiyomaru to us?" Sekiya assisted. "That was the original plan, after all. More importantly, have you arrested Ninagawa yet? Making Takaoki Ninagawa take back the bounty should be your first priority."

Takamine laughed bitterly, as if he didn't need to be told by the likes of Sekiya. "There are political considerations. It's not that simple."

His words hinted at the direct involvement of pols. Perhaps Ninagawa was getting results from throwing massive amounts of money at Nagata-cho, where the Diet, the Prime Minister's office, and various party headquarters were concentrated.

Takamine turned to look coldly at Okumura. "More importantly, how are you planning on transporting Kiyomaru?"

"Only the bullet train will do," the detective declared. "It should be easy so long as no one leaks info. On the bullet train, it should only take around five hours to reach Tokyo."

"But the closest bullet train station from here is New Shimonoseki, where only the Kodama stops," Sekiya told Okumura.

The local Kodama didn't run as often and at most, would only take them to New Osaka. The terminus was usually Hiroshima or Okayama.

If they could get on a Nozomi super express at New Yamaguchi two stations down, they'd have a straight route to Tokyo.

Even if they were to transfer at New Osaka, the Kodama would stop at all bullet train stations along the way. Taking a Hikari express from New Yamaguchi would halve their travel time.

It appeared that Sekiya had done some homework based on the initial plan involving just the transfer team.

Boarding at New Shimonoseki and changing trains at New Yamaguchi chanced that many more people spotting Kiyomaru. According to Sekiya, even if it was slightly farther from Dan-no-Ura PA, speeding down to New Yamaguchi in patrol cars was the smarter move.

Okumura accepted the plan.

Mekari stood up again to say, "I have a request for Senior Superintendent Takamine."

Takamine eyed him warily.

"Even after we depart for New Yamaguchi, please continue to have the transfer force file down the Chugoku Expressway as planned."

Takamine seemed to grasp Mekari's line of thinking immediately.

As it was, the plan for a massive transfer under NPA auspices would be branded a failure. But if the convoy continued to run absent Kiyomaru, they could still receive credit for acting as a diversion to misdirect the masses.

If the team could transfer Kiyomaru via bullet train while the Kiyomaru Site still displayed the location of the transfer force, the risk would be kept at a minimum.

After discussing amongst themselves, the NPA trio came to a decision. While they'd weigh the adverse effects of blocking the inbound side and causing major congestion on the outbound lanes, they'd run the transfer force through to neighboring Hiroshima prefecture, or even Okayama.

In addition to the Yamaguchi Police's black-and-white cruiser, a domestic four wheel drive that had been on standby as the transfer force's rearguard was parked alongside Mekari and company's large transport.

Shiraiwa and Sekiya were going to New Yamaguchi ahead of the rest of them in order to assess the situation and to arrange for a train.

Boomerang-shaped patrol light spinning and siren wailing out, the black-and-white cruiser rumbled off with the two.

The challenge was getting Kiyomaru onto the four wheel drive without providing visuals to the helicopters overhead. That would ruin their plan.

They decided to pull both the transport and the four wheel drive up to the PA's bathrooms. The building had long eaves extending over the entrance, and with a vehicle parked directly in front, there was no fear of being noticed by the helicopters in the sky.

In Shiraiwa's place, Kanbashi took point and went in to inspect the interior. Then Mekari disembarked along with Kiyomaru, followed by Okumura and the NPA trio.

While Kiyomaru was actually relieving himself, the large transport joined up with the Yamaguchi Police's convoy.

The 4WD slipped to the front of the entrance.

The driver's demeanor set Mekari on edge.

The man was feigning calm, but his eyes darted all over the place.

Mekari drew his SIG.

Kanbashi opened the door on the passenger's side and got in. Mekari and Okumura sandwiched Kiyomaru from the front and back and approached the car.

Mekari opened the rear door. The driver locked his gaze on Kiyomaru and shuffled his right hand under his jacket.

When he tried to swivel around, the point of Kanbashi's New Nambu dug into his cheek.

"If you really want a billion, try praying for a miracle," advised the MPD detective.

The driver's trembling right hand let go of the gun at his waist, and he slowly raised both arms.

Witnessing the whole exchange, the NPA trio froze.

Kanbashi used his left hand to yank out the driver's gun and stuck it under his own belt.

Mekari had Okumura sit first in the back seat before ushering in Kiyomaru. Then, carefully checking his surroundings, he entered last and closed the door behind him.

Kanbashi poked the driver's head with the point of his New Nambu.

"Say, how about we get going. Make one suspicious move and I'll blow off your noggin."

With a rickety nod, the driver started the car.

The three honchos stood helplessly by the bathroom building.

Kanbashi showed no sign of putting away the New Nambu.

As a result, Mekari couldn't holster his SIG, either.

A civilian's attempt he could easily fend off. Only cops scared him.

The transfer team included.

Chapter 3

Five People

1

The 4WD descended the Shimonoseki IC and got on National Route 2.

Japan Railways' New Yamaguchi Station was located in Ogori Township. Once called Ogori Station, in 2003 it was renamed New Yamaguchi. It was approximately fifty kilometers from Danno-Ura PA.

It wasn't too busy on National Route 2. Nothing they couldn't zip through by blasting their siren, even if they did get into a jam.

Having split with the army of riot police, Mekari felt himself relax a few notches.

Letting one of them get off a couple of shots was clearly on him. He'd foreseen an attempt on Kiyomaru coming from among the riot police. Still, a battalion of three hundred and fifty had been deployed to protect Kiyomaru. It was difficult to treat every one of their number as a potential threat.

Perhaps, some part of Mekari felt bad about casting undue suspicion on fellow officers—tasked with the same undesirable mission of protecting a child killer—who were nevertheless faithfully doing their jobs.

Had he been naive? It was as if his naïveté had created an

opening. He'd paid the price by acting as Kiyomaru's shield despite himself.

If the assault had been perpetrated by more than one riot policeman, Mekari believed he wouldn't have been able to protect Kiyomaru. And if the suspect had bitten it, chances were that Mekari would have gone down first.

But from here on out, there'd be no riot police. He could assume that anyone who accosted them was a bogey. An SP like Mekari didn't find being on the alert that way too daunting.

They had left the Dan-no-Ura PA at approximately 10:20 a.m. At their current pace, they would probably reach New Yamaguchi in around an hour. If they got on a mid-day bullet train, they'd arrive in Tokyo before five in the afternoon. From Tokyo Station, it was only a short ways to the Metropolitan Police Headquarters in Kasumigaseki.

As long as the world was focused on the transfer force that continued to run down the highway, the chances of them getting attacked was relatively low.

Provided that no one from the transfer team tried to kill Kiyomaru.

Of course the possibility was there, but it seemed manageable.

Shiraiwa attacking Kiyomaru was hard to imagine. Mekari thought he had a good feel for the kind of man Shiraiwa was given their time together.

He'd just met Sekiya, but the man didn't feel dangerous, either.

There was no contempt in Sekiya's eyes when he looked at

Kiyomaru. He was more like a Phys Ed teacher who was popular with his students than a cop. He seemed so stress-free, with no darkness clouding his expression or voice. It was unthinkable that he was hiding an intent to murder their charge.

On the contrary, Okumura was hard to read. While he had a calm demeanor, he combined that with a certain severity. He came across to Mekari like someone who could become a hero or a villain depending on the situation and who he was dealing with. But he didn't seem the type who'd kill for money.

It was Kanbashi who needed to be watched. He easily got riled up, and he also clearly despised Kiyomaru. Whether or not he planned to at the moment, some trivial matter might make him explode and murder Kiyomaru.

Be that as it may, Mekari was confident that he could protect Kiyomaru by staying glued to him.

He was prepared to shoot Kanbashi if it came to that—even if it meant killing him.

When they arrived at New Yamaguchi, a different black-and-white patrol car from the one Shiraiwa and Sekiya had taken awaited them in the drop-off area.

Contacted by the transfer force, they must have come to arrest the driver who'd tried to attack Kiyomaru.

Yet, the officers in the cruiser couldn't be allowed to get near the suspect. Mekari ordered the 4WD's driver to park the car a short distance away from the black-and-white PC. Okumura and Kanbashi got off and escorted the driver to it.

He didn't resist.

Two uniformed officers had also come out of their vehicle. They saw the detectives approaching and saluted. Okumura and Kanbashi returned a light salute and handed over the driver. One of the uniformed officers handcuffed him and put him in the back seat of the patrol car. Kanbashi entrusted the other officer with the gun he'd taken from the driver.

The cruiser left immediately.

Mekari used his cellphone to let Shiraiwa know of their arrival and got into the 4WD along with Okumura and Kanbashi. Confirming that Kanbashi's New Nambu M60 revolver was back in its holster, Mekari put away his SIG P228.

Sekiya and Shiraiwa came running soon enough. Sekiya got in the empty driver's seat, while Shiraiwa remained outside keeping watch on their surroundings.

"We managed to get the Nozomi headed for Tokyo, leaving at 11:45," Sekiya said. He had secured seats for six people in the economy-class Car 11.

"There weren't any private rooms?" asked Okumura.

Since they needed to prevent Kiyomaru from being seen as much as possible, a compartment was preferable.

"All the ones with private rooms only go to New Osaka."

According to Sekiya, among the current Tokaido-Sanyo bullet trains, only the Hikari Rail Star that ran exclusively in the Sanyo segment came equipped with private rooms. The Hikari Rail Star didn't include a luxury Green Car, but the economy-class Car 8 had four compartments for up to four people each.

The Hikari Rail Star's terminus, however, was New Osaka. They would have to use a Nozomi without private rooms from there, and changing trains risked exposing Kiyomaru to many eyes.

Hence, Sekiya said, he'd chosen a Model 700 Nozomi, which used the same engine car as the Hikari Rail Star.

Unlike the Model 300 or 500 Nozomis, the 700 featured a so-called multipurpose room. It was available to people who were disabled or not feeling well, and to mothers who wanted to nurse. In order to access it, you had to ask the conductor to unlock the door.

After hearing that there was only one multipurpose room on the sixteen-car Nozomi and that it was on Car 11, Okumura seemed convinced and nodded.

Shiraiwa went ahead to the platform to keep a lookout. To limit their amount of time in the station building and their chances of being seen, Mekari and the others would wait in the 4WD until the Nozomi No. 86 slid into the platform.

"Hey, inform the boss."

At Okumura's urging, Kanbashi took out his cell phone. He called the MPD's Investigation Section One.

"It's Kanbashi… Yes, sir, that's the case… Right, no problems so far…"

It appeared the MPD had already been told of the change in transfer methods.

"Yes, and so we'll be getting on the Nozomi No. 86. We should arrive in Tokyo at 16:26."

Mekari looked at Kiyomaru. He was fast asleep.

Whether the guy was thick-skinned or just exhausted, Mekari couldn't say.

"Okay, time to head out," Okumura said, glancing at his watch.

Waking Kiyomaru up, Mekari made him pull the hood of his parka down over his eyes.

The top half of the suspect's face was hidden now. Short of actually peering into his face, Mekari judged, no one would be able to identify him.

The five of them got off the car and headed to the station. Okumura and Kanbashi walked side by side, with Sekiya slightly behind them, and Kiyomaru slightly behind him. Mekari, right behind Kiyomaru, kept an eye on their surroundings as they proceeded.

Perhaps because it was midday on a weekday, there didn't appear to be too many people in the station. No one paid particular attention to Mekari's group.

They passed the ticket gate to the bullet train and got on the escalator. They needed to be especially on guard on stairs and escalators. A mere shove could do the trick.

Just as they got on the platform, the train arrived. They could see Shiraiwa standing in front of the door to Car 11.

The door slid open. It was a bit wider than usual, probably so that passengers in wheelchairs could board as-is.

Shiraiwa stepped in right away. Mekari and the others followed.

Immediately to their left after entering, there was a large door with a keyhole. This was probably the multipurpose room.

The door on the right led to a bathroom for the handicapped. Shiraiwa was checking the interior. After he came out, Mekari put

Kiyomaru in the bathroom and closed the door. Posting Shiraiwa there, Mekari started to inspect their surroundings.

On the other side of the aisle from the multipurpose room was a washstand. Directly ahead was the door to the rest of Car 11's passenger area. There were sets of two seats on the right and three on the left. At a quick glance, the occupancy rate appeared to be no more than twenty or thirty percent. Facing another bathroom for the handicapped at the other end were the common bathrooms.

Beyond that was Car 12. There was a phone booth to the right a short way in, and ahead, the door that led to Car 12's seating space.

The departure bell rang. The outside doors closed and the train began to move.

Sekiya, who had disappeared somewhere, returned with the conductor. Lying that they had someone who felt unwell, he had the conductor unlock the door to the multipurpose room. Mekari entered first.

It was smaller than expected. Only two meters wide and one deep, it was around the same size as the paired bathroom. There was a seat where two people could sit side by side, and in front of that, something like a stool with no arm or backrest. It appeared the seating could fold out flat and serve as a bed together with the stool-like piece.

Exiting the multipurpose room, Mekari called out to Shiraiwa and transferred Kiyomaru to the multipurpose room.

It looked like just the SPs sufficed to defend it. At Mekari's urging, Okumura, Kanbashi, and Sekiya moved to their seats in the passenger area.

Mekari and Shiraiwa decided to take turns standing guard outside the multipurpose room door. Shiraiwa would go first.

Mekari entered the multipurpose room and closed the door. He didn't particularly want to be stuck in a confined room with Kiyomaru, but that was that.

Ensconced on the seat, the fellow was humming some tune.

Doesn't seem quite fair.

Settling for the stool, Mekari took out his cellphone. He wanted to check where the transfer force was at the moment.

He'd bookmarked the Kiyomaru Site on his own cell.

It was around an hour and a half since Mekari and the others had split from the transfer force. Maybe it was entering the prefecture of Hiroshima soon.

The screen displayed the page with the map. Mekari stopped breathing.

He couldn't believe his eyes. Goosebumps rose on both of his arms.

The map showed New Yamaguchi.

The blinking red dot was gradually moving away from the station.

Clearly there'd been a leak.

Someone in the force had to be sharing info with the Ninagawa camp. Kanbashi had contacted MPD Investigation Section One. Was someone at HQ selling the info?

Needless to say, the National Police Agency must also have been updated on the transfer team's actions. Was the person connected with Ninagawa from the NPA?

Mekari didn't know when the Kiyomaru Site had begun displaying their current location. Maybe they'd been lucky not to be attacked in New Yamaguchi.

Either way, the next stop, Hiroshima, was where the danger lay.

2

Mekari exited the multipurpose room and showed Shiraiwa the screen of his cell phone.

"For real?!" In contrast to his casual words, Shiraiwa's face was strained.

Mekari sent Shiraiwa to call the other members and leaned his back against the door to the multipurpose room. He put his hand on the SIG at his waist.

There had to be passengers on the train who were already wise to Kiyomaru's presence. Maybe some had boarded just in order to kill him.

They could be attacked at any moment.

"What the hell?!" Kanbashi shouted as he stormed over.

"Someone's leaking info," Mekari said.

He showed the screen of his phone to Kanbashi as well. The detective was speechless.

It even said "Nozomi No. 86" on the display now, for all to see.

Sekiya, who was peering from over Kanbashi's shoulder, also

looked tense.

Mekari cut the i-mode and put his cell phone away to save power.

"So what do you suppose we should do now?" asked Okumura.

He wasn't the type who let his emotions show. Perhaps he'd seen this coming.

There was no denying that the person leaking information could be among the team. But Okumura and Kanbashi, at least, hadn't left Mekari's sight.

Meanwhile, Sekiya and Shiraiwa had gone on ahead. It was also Sekiya who had chosen this train.

Do I have to see him in a new light?

Either way, Mekari couldn't afford to be playing guessing games at the moment.

"I believe assailants are likely to board at the next stop, Hiroshima," Mekari finally replied to Okumura. "But getting off at Hiroshima to elude them would be dangerous, too. We'd be exposing Kiyomaru to an unknown number of potential attackers."

"If that's the case, we should contact Hiroshima PD and have them blanket the station."

Mekari felt annoyed by Sekiya's words. "I'm sure you're all well aware of this by now, but attacks from policemen, not civilians, pose the greater threat. Are you suggesting we bring Kiyomaru out to a massive crowd of officers armed with guns?"

Sekiya looked away. Maybe he was remembering how Mekari had been shot by a riot squad member.

"Then what do you suggest we do?" asked Kanbashi this time.

"I want everyone to decide. If we're prioritizing Kiyomaru's safety, we ought to keep going on this train. It shouldn't be difficult to protect the multipurpose room with all five of us." Gauging each teammate's reaction, Mekari continued, "But we'd be endangering ourselves. If they attacked with guns in the confined space of this train, there'd be nowhere to run."

The others fell silent. They seemed to have finally realized the fix they were in.

"If you don't want that, we'll order an emergency stop and get out on the tracks. There's no knowing what lies ahead if we do that, though."

"How about throwing Kiyomaru out in the aisle while we hide in here?" Kanbashi said, and it was hard to tell whether he was joking.

No one answered. Silence reigned.

As though to shake off the heavy mood, Sekiya spoke.

"In terms of our mission, we need to prioritize protecting Kiyomaru over ourselves. Hey, we're all wearing bulletproof vests and have handguns. We'll be all right, or rather, we'll have to make it be all right."

Such encouraging words.

Mekari realized that his opinion of Sekiya had already changed. Before, he'd have liked the guy as a cop and a man for thinking positively.

Now, it only sounded as though he were spewing sweet lies.

In the end, no one opposed Sekiya's take. Not that they approved, but it would have been awkward to speak up.

Mekari thought it was better than being surrounded by an army of police.

He lost no time instructing the team on where to position themselves. He had Okumura sit next to Kiyomaru and put Shiraiwa in the multipurpose room with them. Mekari would stand in the aisle with his back to the room's door.

Normally, it was the higher-ranking SP who hugged the target, but having admitted to himself that he wasn't ready to be Kiyomaru's shield, Mekari had no choice but to focus on keeping enemies away. That, and he balked at assigning the more dangerous role to someone under his command.

He had Sekiya stand by the door to Car 11's main passenger area, and Kanbashi on the other side by Car 12.

The transfer team probably wouldn't escape injury in the event of an attack. It was crucial that they didn't let one occur. To that end, they needed to intimidate anyone who approached.

Sekiya and Kanbashi, who came across as heavies, were cut out for it.

Mekari told them to keep their hands on their gun grips so they could draw at any time—and above all, to draw before the opponent.

He'd learned the hard way during the attack by the riot policeman.

An announcement flowed through the train car. JR Hiroshima was near.

The sensation of being shot resurfaced in Mekari.

It wasn't fear.

Humiliation.

He'd had a gun but helplessly taken hits, and that was humiliating.

He remembered Subsection Chief Ohki's words: "Shoot anyone who makes suspicious moves."

Sure I will.

A strange elation seemed to fill Mekari.

Sekiya was repeating to Car 11's passengers through the automatic door that had opened, "Sorry for the inconvenience, but you can't exit from this side. Please use the door on the other side to get off."

The train came to a halt. Mekari stepped toward the entrance facing him.

When the door opened, what appeared to be an elderly couple stood on the platform.

"Police. Please board from another doorway."

At Mekari's words, the elderly couple started walking to the right without complaining. The salaryman type behind them strutted off to the left mumbling something. Though the pair of young women behind him glanced at each other, they also headed to another doorway.

A young man who stood further behind, however, didn't move from the spot. He was gripping something under his jacket.

Caught in Mekari's sharp glare, he suddenly looked frightened and about-faced and ran off.

"How many times do I have to tell you, you can't come through here!" Mekari could hear Kanbashi shouting.

Just then, a group of five, no six men came running their way on the platform.

"You can't board from this door!" Mekari shouted.

When the men ignored him and continued to approach, he drew his SIG.

"Police! Stop!"

Flustered, the men quickly came to a halt. They looked at Mekari with what could be rage or fear in their eyes.

There were still plenty of people on the platform, but they just watched from a distance.

The door closed right in front of Mekari's eyes.

It had felt long, but the brief minute was over. The train once again started moving.

Mekari returned to his position in front of the multipurpose room and put away the SIG. Sekiya turned around to him with a grin as though to say, "See? Easy as cake."

Was the man a fool? The dangerous part lay ahead of them.

Passengers who had boarded somewhere along the sixteen cars would now begin to search around the train for Kiyomaru. Eventually, they would reach this spot.

Just then, the door to Car 12 opened and three men entered.

"Police. Can't pass this way," Kanbashi growled, his right hand on the New Nambu at his waist.

The three men's appearances left no room for doubt that they were yakuza.

"Why?" the mustached man at their head wearing a suit asked.

"Doesn't matter why, I'm telling you to piss off."

"What the fuck did you say?"

The trio advanced on Kanbashi, who pressed the muzzle of his New Nambu to Mustache's forehead.

"Hurry up and go back to your seats."

Two guns were raised to aim at Kanbashi's head as he spat out the words. The guy in a leather coat and sunglasses to the left of Mustache held an automatic, while the skinhead in a bomber jacket to the right had pulled out a revolver.

Mekari had already drawn his SIG and had it pointed at the three men. However, if he shot now, things might not go well for Kanbashi.

"Fucking fantastic, you bastards! Shoot me if you can!" Kanbashi roared. "You'll be bathed in this fucker's brains in return!"

No sooner than he finished, a gunshot rang out.

Kanbashi fell.

Mustache gripped an automatic in his right hand. Smoke rose from it.

Mekari fired four shots in rapid succession. All sound disappeared from his ears. At the edge of his vision, empty bullet casings bounced off the aisle wall.

The three men collapsed on the floor as though folding in on each other.

Mekari had aimed below their waists. Not wanting to kill them, he'd avoided slugging their upper bodies with Silvertips.

Two of the three men stayed down unmoving, possibly from the shock of the impact. But not Skinhead. Still lying face up, he was trying to retrieve the revolver he'd dropped.

"Don't move!" Mekari yelled, but how loud he couldn't tell with his deafened ears.

Skinhead didn't stop. He finally gripped the revolver.

Mekari pointed the SIG at the man's head. To immediately and completely halt a human running on high adrenaline, he had no choice but to destroy the brain, the brain stem, the spinal cord, or some other part of the central nervous system.

He aimed between Skinhead's eyes.

Suddenly, the revolver flew from the man's hand. Kanbashi, still sprawled, had pressed his gun to the base of the guy's shoulder and fired.

Skinhead rolled and writhed on the bloody floor.

Sekiya jumped out from behind Mekari. His own gun pointed at the three men, he kicked away their weapons.

Leaning back against the multipurpose room, Mekari kept an eye on the Car 11 entryway that Sekiya had just left unmanned.

The automatic door opened, and the conductor cautiously peeked in. He'd probably heard the gunshots and come running.

"We've got injured. Please get an ambulance to the nearest station."

The conductor gave a big nod to Mekari's words before running off in a hurry.

The door to the multipurpose room opened slightly and Okumura peered out. Presented with the scene in the hallway, he was speechless.

Kanbashi had been shot. It made Mekari's heart ache.

Now that four people had been injured in a shooting incident on board, the train would cease to run as scheduled. All of the passengers would get off, and Hiroshima Police would conduct an investigation.

What about the transfer team? Will I be held?

The situation was already completely unpredictable for Mekari.

3

A copious amount of blood covered the aisle and had sprayed a good part of the walls. The stench was noxious.

Kanbashi had been shot on the left side of his waist. He'd taken off his jacket and had it pressed against his wound to stem blood loss, but he must have already lost a considerable amount and his face looked pale. If he received adequate treatment right away he'd probably live, but depending on the damage to his bones, he might be needing extensive rehabilitation.

The trio who'd attacked were also bleeding heavily, but they didn't seem to be in any danger of dying, either. Sekiya, Okumura, and Shiraiwa were doing their best to stop their bleeding.

Mekari, alone, stayed put in front of the multipurpose room. It was hard to imagine anyone having the guts to attack with this bloodbath in sight, but there were always idiots who couldn't read the memo. He couldn't let his guard down.

The Nozomi No. 86's next stop was Okayama. However, it was thirty minutes away, so they were making an emergency stop at the closest bullet train station, Mihara.

Mekari didn't feel apprehensive about having just shot his first people. He didn't give a shit about the SP "never fired" legend. If anything, he felt some satisfaction that he'd done so unflinchingly in a situation that called for it.

The elation from before was still with him.

Am I starting to crack? he thought in passing.

When they arrived at JR Mihara, EMS were already on standby on the platform.

Skinhead was put on a stretcher.

Mekari had his hand on his SIG, fully intending to shoot if any of the paramedics made a suspicious move. It'd be too late if he got shot first like Kanbashi. Putting aside that EMS didn't bear firearms.

The injured were carried away one after the other on stretchers. Kanbashi went last.

His face twisted as he struggled to bear the pain. "Hey," he called towards Mekari, "is Kiyomaru worth protecting?"

Mekari couldn't answer.

"Why do we have to put our lives on the line for shit like him?!" the detective spat as they carried him out on the stretcher.

The remaining members of the transfer team were all thinking the same thing.

And so Kanbashi was out of the picture.

Mekari had assumed that all passengers would be asked to get off the Nozomi No. 86 at Mihara, but that wasn't so. According to the conductor, Mihara was a station for the local Kodama, and Nozomi passengers left there would have trouble making their connections. To begin with, the sixteen-car super express was more than the station could handle. As such, the Nozomi No.

86 would continue on to Fukuyama, the bullet train station two stops ahead.

Fukuyama was primarily for the Hikari and Kodama. However, Nozomi trains, if only a few, also stopped at Fukuyama, so the plan was to have the passengers transfer there.

Neither Mihara nor Fukuyama was a planned stop for the Nozomi No. 86. People aiming to kill Kiyomaru wouldn't have gathered at either of the stations.

The true threat, once again, was the police.

There were several uniformed officers on the Mihara Station platform, but none made a move to come closer. Mekari's concern was the number of personnel assembling at Fukuyama, where they would have no choice but to unload Kiyomaru.

Just then, he saw two men drawing near. They were wearing armbands that read "RP"—plainclothes from Hiroshima Police's Railway Police Unit.

The railway police used to be called "railroad security officers" back in the days of state ownership when there had been an "N" in JR. When the massive organization had been partitioned and privatized, the former "JNR staff with legal policing rights" had been incorporated into the force. The current RPs were in charge of crimes that occurred on board not just JR trains, but all local private lines and subways as well.

"We will accompany you to Fukuyama."

Of the two men who embarked, one looked to be in his mid-forties, the other his mid-thirties.

The hull doors closed and the train began to move.

Sekiya explained the situation in response to the railway

police's questions.

"…So you're the one who bathed those three in blood?" the senior, horse-faced RP asked, turning toward Mekari.

Sticking out the palm of his left hand Mekari said, "Please don't come any closer." His right hand was still on his SIG.

"Hah?!" A wrinkle appeared lengthwise down Horse-Face's temple. "What the hell do you mean by that, urh?!"

He took a step in the SP's direction.

Mekari drew his SIG and pointed it at Horse-Face, who audibly gulped.

The younger railway cop's pug-like face also froze as he looked at Mekari.

Okumura moved to stand in front of Horse-Face.

"We've already been attacked multiple times. Including by the police…"

"I get it, I get it! Just put it away already!" Pug told Mekari.

Mekari lowered his gun but didn't holster it.

Horse-Face and Pug looked at him as though he were a lunatic.

They arrived at JR Fukuyama at around 12:50. As soon as the doors rolled open, and following the instructions on the intercom, the passengers started moving.

The announcement recommended taking the Nozomi No. 54 due to depart from Fukuyama at 1:05 p.m. They would arrive in Tokyo at 4:46 p.m., only twenty minutes later than No. 86's initial schedule. If they missed the No. 54, no Nozomi train would be stopping at Fukuyama for another hour.

The two RPs disembarked without giving the transfer team a glance.

There were a couple of dozen police on the platform including the forensics team. The RPs joined and briefed them. What was being said about the transfer team was easy to imagine.

Mekari and the others needed to distance themselves from the Nozomi No. 86 soon, but they couldn't budge until the regular passengers were gone.

A plainclothes drew near. No doubt thanks to the RPs' two cents, he didn't attempt to board without warning and spoke from outside the door.

"I'm with Investigation Section One, Hiroshima Police. Could all of you folks come with us for now?"

The man who spoke looked to be in his late forties and had impressively large earlobes.

Okumura stepped forward. "We're currently in the process of transferring Kiyomaru. I'm afraid we can't oblige."

"Whatcha talking about? You folks were participants in the case," Earlobes said, appalled.

"If you have any concerns, please send them to the Metropolitan Police. Using the proper forms," Okumura said coldly.

"The Metropolitan Police, my ass! Looking down on Hiroshima Police, you shits?!" Earlobes bared his teeth in anger.

"We will treat anyone who tries to hinder us as having designs on Kiyomaru," Mekari stated with his hand still on the SIG at his waist.

"Fine then, do whatcha want. You'll get what's coming for ya!" Earlobes spat before returning to his colleagues.

Though it seemed like Mekari had escaped detainment for now, he couldn't decide how to proceed.

"Mekari, should we be taking the Nozomi No. 54 too?" Okumura asked.

"I'd like us to, but if info keeps on leaking, we're toast."

"Next time one of us might die," Sekiya said with forced light-heartedness.

No matter how it was worded, it was the truth.

"Shouldn't we just call it off? The situation's gone too foul," Shiraiwa spoke up for the first time in a while.

"Scared?" Okumura said as though to get a rise out of the SP sergeant.

"It just feels stupid, you know? It's exactly as Mr. Kanbashi said. Why do we have to put our lives on the line for Kiyomaru?"

"That's absolutely right. Any of you want to drop out, go ahead. I won't stop you," Okumura offered, his face stern.

Shiraiwa looked as though he wanted to say something, but swallowing his words, he took out his cell phone.

Calling it off had never crossed Mekari's mind.

To be honest, he didn't give a damn about Kiyomaru.

Mekari had been shot for the first time today. He'd shot others for the first time as well. After all that, he couldn't leave this mission hanging.

"As long as none of us contacts anyone, there's no way info could leak, is there?" said Sekiya, who appeared to have no intention of stepping down, either.

"We can't make the gentlemen from Hiroshima Police wait on the platform forever, can we," Okumura pressed Mekari for a decision.

Fukuyama, like Mihara, had only one set of tracks each for inbound and outbound bullet trains, so they couldn't let the Nozomi stay put. In order to inspect the scene, Hiroshima Police would be moving the Nozomi No. 86 somewhere where it could be parked.

Making the Hiroshima Police wait didn't bother Mekari the least bit, but it was risky to remain in one place for too long.

"Mr. Mekari…"

Shiraiwa held out his cell phone. It was hard to say if he looked angry or frightened. Okumura and Sekiya also drew near to peer into the screen.

The blinking red dot on display was hovering at Fukuyama Station.

Mekari had been prepared. Still, he was shaken.

Where did they get their info?

The Nozomi No. 86 was parked at a station that was not on its itinerary, and no one on the transfer team had contacted anyone. Not a single one of them had worked solo this time. Was it the Hiroshima Police?

But they didn't have the time to stop and ponder. If Kiyomaru's location had been identified as Fukuyama Station by the website, they needed to move as quickly as possible.

"Let's take the Nozomi No. 54."

Mekari opened the door to the multipurpose room.

Escorted out by Shiraiwa, Kiyomaru paused and stared at the massive amount of blood on the floor. They could see his own draining from his face.

Glancing around the transfer team, he asked, "Did that short-fused copper die?" His flippant tone was clearly a facade.

No one answered him.

Mekari led as the four surrounded Kiyomaru and bid farewell to the Nozomi No. 86. The glaring local cops almost seemed murderous, but not one of them tried to approach. Instead, they rushed into the space the transfer team had just left.

With Hiroshima Police on board, No. 86 slowly pulled out of the station.

The Nozomi No. 54 left Fukuyama ten minutes behind schedule.

Since it was another Model 700, they put Kiyomaru in the multipurpose room again, and Mekari stood outside the door. Sekiya took the Car 11 side, Okumura the Car 12 side. In front of the boarding entrance, Shiraiwa was gazing at the screen of his cell phone.

Mekari pulled out his SIG. He exchanged the magazine, now missing four shots, with one of the full spares before returning the gun to its holster.

Shiraiwa silently thrust his cell phone towards Mekari. The blinking red light on the screen was slowly pulling out of Fukuyama Station.

The Ninagawa camp was indeed privy to the transfer team's every movement.

There was a chance that Hiroshima PD had gotten wind of the switch. But if one of their investigators had reported to prefectural headquarters, which in turn had tipped off the NPA or MPD, from where the info had been relayed to the Ninagawa camp, then the website's reaction time was a tad too impressive. It was also hard to believe that Hiroshima Police had direct ties with the Ninagawa camp.

Okumura said out of the blue, "I'm afraid we're being tailed by Public Security."

"Ah," Mekari couldn't but let out. A chill ran down his spine.

4

Public Security.

Mekari felt as though a foggy mental image had come into focus. Come to think of it, would the National Police Agency's Security Division, the crux of law and order in Japan, ever entrust the transfer to just Mekari and a few other cops?

At least since New Yamaguchi, a substantial Public Security operation must have been giving detailed reports.

He hadn't noticed at all. But perhaps it was no surprise that he hadn't. After all, this was Public Security, the pros at collecting info, who monitored, stalked, wiretapped, and brainwashed to get what they needed.

With the NPA Security Division as the apex, Public Security Police investigated and gathered intelligence on "crimes that impinged on national security." Along with the Security Planning, Security, and Foreign Affairs sections, the Security Division was host to Public Security Sections One, Two, and Three.

Public Security Section One gathered intel on mass-movement organizations such as labor unions, with the Communist

Party being their main target. They also handled info regarding the Aum Shinrikyo cult.

Section Two did the same mostly for right-wing organizations.

Section Three handled the "extreme-left violent groups," or New Left sects like the National Committee and the Revolutionary Marxists.

All of the prefectural police departments had their own public security section, but because the budget came from the national treasury, PSP across Japan were in fact under the direct control of the NPA Security Division. In other words, info obtained by its investigators was sent directly to the NPA, and local police couldn't interfere. The investigators sometimes even casually acted outside of their jurisdiction.

As an arm of the Japanese police organization, Public Security was shrouded in mystery. It divulged no details whatsoever about its runaway headcount or funding. The investigators hid that they were "Public Security" from other police, let alone civilians, it was said. The force was thorough with the secrecy on this point.

Mekari thought that if the transfer team really was being tailed by Public Security, it might be impossible to lose them. Of course, tailing wasn't a unique technique and came into play in investigations of normal criminal cases. Yet, because Public Security mostly tracked activists who were ever suspicious of being followed, the amount of care and precision put into the task was in a league of its own. In addition to combining various methods like "direct column tailing," "parallel column tailing," "circulation tailing," and "angular tailing," they went for complex maneuvers like overtaking or lying in wait, not to mention switching out personnel to avoid notice. For important targets, it wasn't rare for several dozen agents to be involved.

For the current situation, new faces might have partaken in the mission at every train stop. The transfer team was possibly being monitored by a few hundred Public Security personnel all told.

The intel would be sent directly to the NPA Security Division and relayed to the Ninagawa camp from there. If someone among the brass was connected with Ninagawa, then plugging the leak was impossible. In order to transfer Kiyomaru safely, they had to either bring down the website or arrest Ninagawa. Neither of those things, however, was likely to happen today or tomorrow.

Just then, Mekari's cell phone buzzed in his pocket. Taking it out, he saw that the call was from the MPD Security Section.

"It's Ishibashi…"

The superintendent was the administrator for the mobile security contingent.

"We just heard from Hiroshima Police that an officer was shot. Who?"

"Kanbashi from Investigation Section One. It wasn't fatal. They've already taken him to a hospital from Mihara Station."

"I see… and where are you guys now?"

"Exactly where the Kiyomaru Site says we are."

A faint groan came from the other end of the line.

After a brief pause, Administrator Ishibashi spoke again, in a gentler tone.

"Are you all right?"

"..."

Mekari couldn't reply. Should he have said, "I'm fine, sir" and thumped his chest? Or maybe screamed, "There's no way in hell we're all right"?

"Regarding the leaks, we're working with Investigation Section One to come up with a countermeasure. In the meantime, do you think you guys could wait somewhere safe?"

Mekari almost cracked up. "If you tell me where, sir."

It was Ishibashi's turn to fall silent.

"Being on the move beats staying put and waiting for people who're after Kiyomaru to come to us in droves."

"..."

"Instead, can you hurry up and at least take down the mobile site, if not the PC one?"

"We've been working with every cell phone company, but it goes right back up every time we crush it. The longest we've been able to keep it down was close to seven minutes. It usually goes back up in less than two minutes."

Mekari wasn't surprised. This was Ninagawa's camp, and they wouldn't drop the ball. Generous sums must have found their way to the cell phone companies as well.

"Then please worry instead about when we get there. It'd suck to put our lives on the line and deliver Kiyomaru just to see him get killed at HQ."

Done venting, Mekari cut off the call. Speaking to someone who had no clue about how things were on the ground was a waste of time.

The next hoop, Okayama Station, was fast approaching.

They arrived at JR Okayama fifteen minutes or so after boarding the Nozomi No. 54. Passengers getting off were forming a line in the aisle outside the multipurpose room.

Taking to heart how Kanbashi had gotten shot, Mekari was trying out a different method. At Hiroshima, he'd hoped cops with guns would be intimidating enough to prevent anyone from coming near the multipurpose room. The result had been a shootout.

The transfer team couldn't afford to lose another member.

Even if the whole world knew that Kiyomaru was aboard the Nozomi No. 54, the site wasn't so specific as to display the car number. Maybe not tipping people off was wiser. As long as Kiyomaru stayed in the multipurpose room, he couldn't be assaulted except by firearms, and there couldn't be that many attackers who owned them. At the same time, letting a crowd of people near the room was dangerous, no doubt. There was no telling what might happen.

In a way, this was a gamble.

Mekari and Shiraiwa stood beside the multipurpose room, by the door that wouldn't open at the station. If the passengers were to move by smoothly, the team couldn't stand in the aisle. Sekiya was watching Car 11's seating area, and Okumura Car 12's. There was only a limited amount of space around the multipurpose room, and if the four of them stood clumped together, they'd only hinder each other's movements.

Both Mekari and Shiraiwa had drawn their SIGs. They hid

their right hands gripping the SIGs under their jackets so regular passengers wouldn't notice.

"Go for a headshot if anyone points a gun at us," Mekari had ordered Shiraiwa.

Adrenaline would be coursing through someone ready to commit a crime. A high rush made people temporarily immune to pain; the same thing happened with drug or alcohol use. Adrenaline, moreover, had the function of elevating aggression. There were plenty of cases reported overseas of perps pumped full of lead coolly continuing with their shooting sprees. Apparently, humans were capable of taking action for up to ninety seconds even after their hearts were damaged.

Getting shot point-blank in the narrow car, which offered zero cover, spelled death. An attack on their current location meant that the gun in the assailant's outstretched hand would be just a few dozen centimeters away. If the shot didn't completely neutralize the threat, managing to fire first didn't cut it. The assailant could easily get off a shot even as he fell and hit either Shiraiwa or Mekari in the face.

They had to destroy the central nervous system to avoid coming under fire. There was no other way to protect themselves, as it were.

The exit door opened.

The passengers lined up in the aisle disembarked in a steady stream. In turn, fresh passengers boarded one after the other. Some were obviously benign, others not so. There were people who seemed oddly nervous, and others who paid too much attention to Mekari and Shiraiwa's gazes.

Mekari stared at the passengers without even blinking. They were moving in more or less smoothly.

A thirtysomething couple with a baby came on carrying some large piece of luggage.

The father immediately placed it in the aisle and crouched down. The mother, who held the baby, stood right in front of Mekari and Shiraiwa. Her husband was trying to pull something out of the many pockets lining the outside of the bag.

The other passengers brushed past them.

Mekari called out to the father, "Please move along."

The man glanced at Mekari, made an annoyed face, and continued to root through the bag's pockets.

Mekari thrust the SIG in front of the man's face.

"Please move along."

The father gulped. The mother almost fell over backwards together with the baby, but Shiraiwa caught her from behind. He looked at Mekari as if to say, "That's taking it too far."

Dragging their bag, the couple with the baby fled to the seats.

A well-built young man who'd been standing directly behind the mother pulled out a long sashimi knife from under his jacket.

He jabbed its tip towards Mekari's face.

"Where's Kiyomaru?!" he demanded, his voice shaking.

See, an idiot.

He'd brought a knife to a gunfight. His mind was most likely blank with panic.

Shiraiwa aimed his SIG at the man's face and said, "Get off."

The man stared down the deep, 9 millimeter-wide hole, frozen in shock.

Shiraiwa repeated himself. "Get off. Else I'll shoot to kill."

He looked like he'd really do it.

The Knife Guy leapt out of the train.

The area surrounding the multipurpose room was already devoid of passengers. The hull door closed, and the train lurched into motion.

Mekari felt like they might be able to protect Kiyomaru without further injury to the transfer team this way.

He doubted anyone would just massacre them before assaulting Kiyomaru. Killing multiple persons resulted in the death penalty. A billion yen meant nothing if you were sentenced to death.

For the same reason, it was hard to imagine that anyone would try to derail the train. Even if several hundred people died, there was no guarantee that Kiyomaru would die, while the perp would most certainly face capital punishment.

The sort of person who didn't mind dying if it meant leaving money behind for family probably wouldn't plan on mass murder. That was the province of leftist or religious terror, but such a scenario was beyond Mekari's pay grade. It was exactly the kind of thing that Public Security needed to handle.

"This feels kind of doable, doesn't it?"

Shiraiwa was smiling for the first time in a while.

Mekari shook his head. Even if they were able to protect Kiyomaru without getting anyone on the team hurt, if an attacker had a gun they'd have no choice but to fire. The assailant would either die or be wounded critically. Then the train would stop, and the team and Kiyomaru would have to get off and switch again. It didn't seem like they could pull that off too many times.

Worse, if they had to shoot every time they were attacked, there was no way the transfer wouldn't be suspended.

They simply had to prevent any further attacks on Kiyomaru. Yet, people with guns could be drawing near even as they spoke.

Footsteps came from the direction of Car 12. Shiraiwa stiffened and turned around.

It was Okumura.

"The conductor just told me something. He says it's a fiasco at New Kobe."

Apparently, a large number of people had gathered on the platform where the Nozomi No. 54 would stop at New Kobe, the next station. A JR staff member managing the gawkers had been shoved onto the tracks. The police had come running and gotten into a scuffle with the crowd, and sensing danger, one of the officers had fired a warning shot. The platform was already in a state of chaos.

"As a result, the train will be skipping New Kobe and continuing on to New Osaka."

At JR West Japan's request, the Osaka Riot Police had been dispatched to stand guard at the station.

"They're also telling us to get off at New Osaka with Kiyomaru."

Their reasoning was that they could no longer guarantee the safe operation of the bullet trains.

"I asked what would happen if we refused, just to be told that this train simply won't leave New Osaka until we get off."

It was obvious they'd get nowhere defying JR's wishes.

Neither Mekari nor Shiraiwa said a word.

They would have to unload Kiyomaru at a huge station like New Osaka—straight into several hundred riot police who awaited.

5

So it was impossible after all. Mekari felt overwhelmed by despair.

Transferring Kiyomaru via bullet train was premised on their whereabouts being unknown. Given that their location was public knowledge, taking an ordinary passenger train had been an open invitation to a stream of attackers. But no alternative came to mind.

Even if they could board a plane or ship, it was hardly an enticing proposition. There'd be nowhere to run in the event of an attack. Fleeing would equal death.

As for cars, it was clear as day that they'd end up in a traffic jam if their position wasn't secret. Someone rear-ending them was all it would take for the mission to be halted. Getting hemmed in by a crowd in the cramped space of a vehicle was no way to guard Kiyomaru.

Of all their options the bullet train had seemed the best, but now that was coming to an end.

Riot police were deployed at New Osaka. If they tried to attack, there was not much the team could do. Those guys were tough, wore helmets and armored vests, and carried guns.

A charging squad member might be downed with a shot to the lower body, but if he continued to fire, there was no way to stop him. His central nervous system couldn't be taken out, his head protected by a helmet and protective visor. The Silvertips loaded into the SPs' SIGs had low penetrative force and were sadly ineffective against helmets and body armor.

When Mekari had been shot, there had only been one riot policeman against the five transfer team members in the large transport.

How about facing several hundred?

Ninety-nine percent of them were working earnestly to uphold law and order. They wouldn't dream of killing Kiyomaru even for a billion yen.

But Mekari feared the remaining one percent.

One percent of several hundred would be several people. If they attacked simultaneously, or consecutively, he didn't think they'd be able to protect Kiyomaru. There was no way to know which ones among the several hundred would attack and when, and keeping an eye on the actions of all the riot police present was beyond impractical.

The transfer team could suffer fatalities if they were to safeguard the suspect through it all. Mekari didn't believe it was right for any other human being to die in Kiyomaru's place. If someone had to die, that someone was Kiyomaru himself.

Yet his death meant victory for Ninagawa.

That was intolerable.

If the man thought throwing money around could make everything go his way, he was badly mistaken. Mekari wanted to prove that to Ninagawa.

Should they bring the train to an emergency halt and get off before reaching New Osaka?

That was the only option if they wanted to avoid the riot police, but the Nozomi No. 54's crew would decline to cooperate. The team didn't want to get off at a place with riot police, so the train had to stop? They wouldn't see why. Nor could they be made to comply at gunpoint. If Mekari did that, he'd simply get arrested, and the transfer would be aborted.

No matter how much he thought about it, there was no way out. Mekari steeled himself, his luck in heaven's hands.

He explained to the rest of the transfer team the dangers posed by New Osaka. They all looked tense, but no other path offered itself.

Each of them was free to act as he saw fit in the case of an attack. Maybe running away was the correct choice here. None of them wanted to protect Kiyomaru badly enough to lay down their lives. It wasn't as though they were being paid that much. To begin with, they couldn't even trust the police organization itself anymore. No one could blame them if they ditched the mission.

JR New Osaka was approaching. The Nozomi No. 54 was entering Track 26.

Mekari couldn't believe his eyes.

There was no one on the platform at all.

The conductor came. He probably needed to confirm that Kiyomaru and the team were making themselves scarce at New Osaka. The intercom repeatedly instructed Car 11 passengers getting off at the station to use the exit on the Car 10 side.

They stopped and the doors opened. Passengers descended

to the platform one after another. Thanks to the announcement, none tried to pass in front of the multipurpose room.

"Where are the riot police?" Mekari asked the conductor.

According to him, when the squads had arrived, the platform had been overflowing with people. Adding several hundred more bodies to provide security was judged to be untenable. Instead, they'd moved everyone off the platform and positioned the personnel in the lower bullet train concourse. They were currently blocking the passage to Tracks 25 and 26.

Because most of Nozomi No. 86's passengers had transferred to Nozomi No. 54, the train was already pretty crowded. In light of this, JR Tokai had decided not to allow new passengers to board at New Osaka.

The transfer team didn't have to face danger the moment they got off, at least. But they couldn't let their guards down. After setting foot on the platform, they'd have nowhere to go. Whether they were leaving the station or moving to a different track, they'd be descending into a throng of riot police. Once most of the passengers transited through, they were to leave the train with Kiyomaru. They didn't have any time to think.

Mekari entrusted the multipurpose room to Shiraiwa and got off onto the platform. He somehow had to find an escape route. There was sure to be a service passageway for JR staff and vendors. He weaved between the people headed towards the stairs and escalators.

Eight-car Hikari Rail Stars were on both Tracks 24 and 25, exactly eight cars off from each other. They'd most likely been parked there for the time being to hide the sixteen-car Nozomi

No. 54 from the other platforms.

Just then, out of the corner of his eye, Mekari saw a man clamber up onto the platform from Track 25.

The man who now stood on the platform held a revolver in his right hand. He looked around and made for the Nozomi No. 54.

Mekari drew his SIG. He cocked the hammer with his right thumb.

The SIG didn't have a "safety" in the usual sense of the word, no mechanism that prevented it from firing. It simply had a lever that knocked the hammer to a safe spot away from its firing position, and the hammer stayed there while the gun was being carried around. To fire, all you needed to do was point the muzzle and firmly squeeze the trigger. For the first shot, however, pulling the trigger also served to raise the hammer. The extra force required, compared to the shots that followed, meant that the muzzle tended to jerk. For the first shot to aim true, you needed to cock the hammer manually with your thumb.

In order to spare the innocent bystanders on the platform, Mekari had to down the man with one bullet.

"Stop! Police!"

At his voice, the man turned around bodily and pointed his revolver at Mekari. They were approximately eight meters apart.

Mekari aimed for the hip bone and fired.

When the pelvis was shattered, the human body could no longer sustain its weight and toppled without fail.

The man shook before falling backwards onto his posterior. Any further resistance and Mekari would have to shoot him in the head.

The mental blow of getting shot, however, seemed to have sapped his will to fight. He threw away his revolver and raised both arms off the platform.

Mekari kept the SIG pointed at the man and approached cautiously, scanning their surroundings and checking for other potential aggressors.

Everyone in the vicinity stood frozen in shock.

He crouched and picked up the dropped revolver. It was a Brazilian .38 caliber.

That was when, again out of the corner of his eye, he saw a man crawl up from the tracks onto the platform. This one had a large kitchen knife gripped in his right hand.

Look, another idiot.

Hadn't he seen the other man get shot? It beat Mekari how he had the nerve to come up armed with just a knife.

"Police! Don't move!"

The man ignored Mekari and burst into a sprint.

"Stop! I'll shoot!"

Despite his words, Mekari couldn't just fire at someone who didn't have a gun.

The man ran towards a mother and her children who stood watching, frozen by the report.

Mekari pointed his gun upwards and fired a warning shot. People hastily ducked down around him.

The man didn't falter, though. He grabbed one of the children, a girl of about five, and placed the knife against her neck.

"Where's Kiyomaru?! Bring him out!"

Sitting down as though her knees had given out, the mother clutched the elementary-age boy next to her—probably the older brother of the girl who'd been taken hostage.

His SIG aimed at the man, Mekari approached warily.

The guy kept the knife pressed to the girl's throat as he turned to face Mekari.

"Stay away! I'll kill this kid!"

The mother screamed. The girl began to cry loudly.

The hand holding the knife was shaking. It was unclear whether it was from adrenaline or fear, but he was obviously a complete amateur at this. A plump man who looked to be in his late fifties.

"Hurry up and bring out Kiyomaru! I'm serious, I'm absolutely serious!"

The man wore a light jacket over his work clothes. The very image of the owner of a small factory or hardware store, he had a broad forehead, and his hair had thinned out quite a bit. He looked neither tough nor violent. An ordinary citizen in dire straits.

"Don't you care what happens to this kid?! I'll do it, I really will!"

His eyes were bloodshot. He may have downed a few to give himself courage.

Though Mekari felt bad for the girl who'd been taken hostage, he had no time to spare on guys like these.

Ready to return to the multipurpose room, he turned his back to the hostage-taker. Sekiya was almost directly behind him.

A variety of obstacles blocked the view from where the room

was. The Fukuoka cop couldn't have seen any of it, but he'd heard the gunshot and most likely come to investigate.

He gently called out to the perp, "Put down the knife, okay?"

"Stop," Mekari said, grabbing him by the shoulder. "Don't get involved."

"We can't just abandon the kid."

"It's not our job."

Sekiya's expression changed. "Then go call the riot police!!"

It was a fearsome look Mekari hadn't seen on him until now.

6

There was no time to be arguing with Sekiya. Mekari ran back to the multipurpose room.

"A girl's been taken hostage. The criminal demands Kiyoma-ru."

Okumura and Shiraiwa gulped, and something like a scream escaped the conductor's throat.

Mekari said to Okumura, "At this rate, the riot police will come up. Please stop them somehow."

"Right, I'll tell them it's one of the perp's terms…"

Okumura broke into a sprint towards the stairs.

True, the riot police would balk if they were told that the perp was threatening to kill the hostage if he saw any police. But there was no knowing how long.

"Please get off now. Immediately. This train will be pulling out!" the conductor yelled hysterically.

"You turning us out when we're going through this?!" Shiraiwa rounded on him.

"What if the criminal boards?! It'll turn into a bullet train hijacking!!"

The conductor was quite right. Mekari opened the door to the multipurpose room and brought out Kiyomaru, who had no idea what was going on and looked spaced out.

SIGs in hand, Mekari and Shiraiwa kept close watch on their surroundings as they unloaded Kiyomaru onto the platform.

The door closed behind them right away. Making Kiyomaru stand with his back toward the stainless steel hull, Mekari and Shiraiwa flanked him.

The Nozomi No. 54 slowly slid into motion.

Mekari was stuck. At least until Sekiya and Okumura returned, he couldn't leave Kiyomaru to Shiraiwa alone and go look for an escape route.

Was Sekiya still trying to talk down the perp? He might eventually succeed, but it could take hours. They couldn't afford to waste that much time.

Okumura came jogging back. "The riot police will hold back for now. But you need to be prepared for plainclothes from Osaka Police to come up sooner or later."

That made sense. As far as Mekari was concerned, the local police could come handle the hostage situation asap so they could leave the platform.

Sekiya returned. His expression was grim.

"We've got to show him Kiyomaru."

Mekari couldn't understand what Sekiya was saying.

"He's half crazed now that the train's left. He's assuming Kiyomaru left too, and he's about to lose it. I think the situation's really dangerous. I'm saying let's show him Kiyomaru's still here to calm him down."

"That's impossible. We can't expose Kiyomaru to danger," Mekari said firmly.

"The man only has a knife. Kiyomaru won't be in any danger."

"If we do that, we won't be able to move until the hostage situation's resolved."

"The perp's saying he'll kill the girl if Kiyomaru's gone!"

"Our mission is to guard and transfer Kiyomaru."

"Mekari, let's bring him to the perp," Okumura interrupted. "It might be okay for you SP to only ever care about the VIP, but we detectives can't ignore a crime occurring before our eyes."

"Cops fulfill their assigned roles," Mekari said, drawing closer to Okumura.

"If it means leaving that kid to die, fuck being a cop!" Sekiya spat.

Okumura and Sekiya each took one of Kiyomaru's arms and began to haul him away. Shiraiwa followed.

"I'm saying we should prioritize our mission!" Mekari insisted.

Okumura looked back. "Is Kiyomaru's life so important?"

Is Kiyomaru's life so important?

What was the man saying, at this late stage? Who cared about Kiyomaru's life? What was his point?

Mekari felt so frustrated that he wanted to scream.

Kiyomaru turned to look at Mekari but didn't say anything.

He put up no resistance as he was taken away. Mekari had no choice but to follow.

The number of passengers remaining on the platform had diminished to the point where they could be counted. They were watching the hostage situation unfold from a safe distance.

Among the bystanders, no doubt, were Public Security personnel. But it looked like they weren't involving themselves in the hostage case. They probably had no intention of dealing with anything beyond their assigned mission. Mekari wished Okumura and Sekiya would take a hint from them.

EMS had arrived. They were carrying away the man who'd been shot. Mekari also caught a glimpse of several uniformed officers hiding in the stairs and keeping an eye on the hostage situation.

Still holding the knife to the girl's neck, the man had his back to the elevator. Mekari could hear the sobs of the mother, who sat there next to the perp. The boy, around ten, stood as though to defend her, his hands curled into fists and his mouth a rigid line.

Sekiya and Okumura stopped. Kiyomaru, Shiraiwa, and Mekari did too.

They were several meters from the hostage-taker. Kiyomaru stood in the center, with Mekari and Okumura to his left and right, Sekiya in the front, and Shiraiwa to the rear.

An attack from behind, where Track 26 lay, was unlikely. The same went for direct fire from the stairs, thanks to vending machines and such serving as cover.

As Sekiya had predicted, the hostage-taker's panic appeared to abate a little at the sight of Kiyomaru. In contrast to the man's relieved expression, the girl's face was sheet white, and her breathing was unnaturally fast. She looked like she was already on the verge of passing out. Perhaps the extreme stress had caused her to hyperventilate.

Mekari's heart ached at the sight of the girl. He remembered the faces of Megumi Nishino and Chika Ninagawa that he'd seen on the news. Two girls who'd been butchered by Kiyomaru.

Sizing up the hostage, Kiyomaru spoke.

"Hah, the brat's ugly…"

Sekiya turned around and punched him in the face in one motion. It was a shattering blow.

Shiraiwa caught Kiyomaru as he fell backwards. A faint smile crossed the guy's face even as he was propped up. The inside of his mouth was crimson. He spat bloody saliva onto the platform.

Let's just kill this guy, Mekari thought quite seriously.

"Bring Kiyomaru over here!" the perp hollered.

"He isn't going anywhere. Let's calm down and talk." Sekiya raised both arms and stepped forward.

"Shut up, idiot! Just hurry up and bring him!"

Mekari was eyeing the elevator behind the man.

What appeared to be a ten-key panel was affixed next to the door. You probably punched in a security code. Was it for vendors bringing in their products?

They might be able to escape past the riot police via the elevator, but there was no knowing where it led. There might be a locked door down where it landed. And if it was for passengers on wheelchairs, it'd take them to the dead center of the bullet train concourse. Into the crowd dammed up by the riot police.

Mekari wanted to know for sure but didn't see any station staff nearby. Either way, they couldn't even approach the elevator while the hostage situation obtained. He had to let it go.

"Sekiya, what do you plan on doing now?" asked Okumura.

"I'm afraid patiently talking him down is the only option…" replied Sekiya, apparently not understanding the question's meaning.

"In any case, Osaka Police will eventually arrive," Okumura explained. "Whether it's railway cops or the mobile investigation unit or Sec One's special crimes people."

"…"

"At that point, Fukuoka Police or the MPD, we won't be wanted here outside of our jurisdiction."

"But…"

"We're moving with Kiyomaru as soon as Osaka Police arrive. You understand that, right?"

Mekari said, "The perp's just one man, with only a knife. Meanwhile, there'll be a few dozen prefectural police investigators, all with guns. You know we can't let them near Kiyomaru."

"But the perp says he'll kill the hostage if Kiyomaru leaves! What if the girl's stabbed the moment we take Kiyomaru away? You'd still take him and go?!"

"Then what do you suggest we do?! Hand the perp Kiyomaru as he demands?!"

Sekiya and Mekari were both getting emotional. Mekari knew that wasn't good, but he couldn't help it. It wasn't as if he didn't mind the hostage girl getting hurt. There just wasn't anything they could do at the moment. This was why they shouldn't have interacted with the perp in the first place.

"Do you think he'll really kill the hostage?" Okumura asked Sekiya.

"I feel like there's a high risk of that happening. The man feels cornered. It wouldn't be beyond him."

"If he kills the hostage, he won't be able to achieve his objective."

"After stabbing the girl, he'll probably take the boy hostage. Then the mother…"

Mekari also sensed that risk. It was hard to imagine that boy or mother abandoning the girl and cutting loose. The perp didn't come across as a savage man and might even have been a good husband and father. But Sekiya was right, there was no telling with cornered amateurs. They didn't realize the weight of their actions until after the fact.

"And what's your plan?" Okumura asked Sekiya once again.

"…"

Sekiya couldn't answer. A sour expression overtook his face.

Just then, they heard the ruckus of a large number of people running up the stairs.

Wearing armbands that said "CIS" and "MIS" on their left arms—the criminal and mobile investigation sections—the men appeared one after the other. Osaka Police cops.

"For now, I'll go talk to them."

Okumura ran in the direction of the stairs.

"Hey! Hurry up and bring Kiyomaru!!" the perp barked again. It seemed that the Osaka Police's arrival was pushing him to the edge.

Sekiya looked at Mekari. "The girl's life and Kiyomaru's life, which is more important?"

This again.

Mekari could only answer: "Both."

"Then, what about that pops?"

"…"

He didn't have a reply to that one. Shiraiwa and Kiyomaru also stared at Sekiya in silence.

Sekiya drew the New Nambu two-inch revolver from the holster at his waist. Keeping his hands relaxed at his sides, he started to walk towards the perp.

"Dammit! What happened to Kiyomaru, idiot?!"

Ignoring the angry shout, Sekiya slowly moved closer.

"Don't come! The hell are you doing?! Want me to kill the brat?!"

"It's not happening. How about you gave up," Sekiya said quietly and inched over.

"I-I'll really do it! I'll really kill her! What do you take me for?!"

"If you even put a scratch on that child, I'll shoot you dead."

Sekiya pointed his gun at the man. The distance between them had already shrunk to three meters.

"What do you think you're doing, dumbass?!" an investigator from the Osaka Police yelled at Sekiya.

With his New Nambu still pointed at the perp, Sekiya stopped.

The girl was breathing as raggedly as before and seemed to be floating in and out of consciousness.

The man looked terrified. His entire face gleamed with sweat. But his eyes were also lit with madness.

"I don't want to kill you. Please just let the kid go…" Sekiya said, almost pleading.

"I-I'm serious. I've nowhere left to turn. Killing Kiyomaru is the only way!" the man said with a trembling voice.

He's here to die, Mekari sensed.

Sekiya moved even closer.

"Please drop the knife…"

"D-Do I really need to stab her? You won't see until I actually kill this…" The man's body was shaking as though he were feverish.

"You probably have family too. Think about your family."

Sekiya pressed forward again. The muzzle of the gun in his outstretched right hand was only around a meter from the man's head.

"Who the fuck do you think I'm doing this for?!" the man howled, losing it.

He raised his knife high.

"Drop your knife!!"

"Nraaaaaahhhh!!!"

A roar issued forth. The mother shrieked.

A dry explosion resounded.

A dark blue hole popped open above the man's left eye. Red mist danced behind his head.

His body was rigid like a stick as it fell back.

Sekiya leapt forward and caught the girl, who'd been thrown aloft.

The back of the man's head collided with the floor. He stared blankly at a point on the ceiling, unmoving.

The air seemed frozen. The platform fell into a hush, with not a voice to be heard. The only sound may have been the girl's labored breathing.

Sekiya handed the girl he held to her mother, who tried to say something to him but had no words. Taking the girl and tightly embracing her, she broke down in tears.

Suddenly the boy also began to cry. He'd been bearing it as best he could, but now tears spilled down his cheeks. His hands still balled, and facing up, he kept on weeping.

Sekiya returned to Mekari and the others. His face was disturbingly blank.

He was panting like he'd been holding his breath the whole time.

"Yo, murderer," Kiyomaru called out to him.

Sekiya pointed his gun at Kiyomaru. "Shall I murder you too?"

Mekari silently placed himself in front of the muzzle.

Sekiya locked eyes with him. Then, he slowly lowered his gun.

Okumura approached with one of the Osaka Police investigators who looked like he might be administrator-class.

"You, what's your section and rank?" the man asked Sekiya.

"Fukuoka Prefectural Police, Criminal Investigation Section One, Sergeant Kenji Sekiya. You're not complaining, are you?"

"That guy was only holding a knife and had yet to hurt anyone. Why did you kill him?"

"…"

"Your course of action clearly deviated from the Police Duties Execution Law. I'm going to have to ask you to come with us."

Sekiya let out a heavy sigh. "Typical."

Mekari couldn't find the right words to say to him. Okumura and Shiraiwa also stared silently at his receding form.

"I saved the hostage. I protected Kiyomaru. What else should I have done?"

Sekiya's loud parting words sounded across the platform.

He was right.

Yet also fundamentally mistaken.

Chapter 4

Three People

1

The site inspection began. Yellow tape was stretched around the area. Strobe lights flashed from the forensics crew non-stop.

The perp's remains had already been carried away. A dark pool of blood indicated where a living human had stood only a short while before.

Mekari explained to the Osaka Police investigators how he'd shot the man with the gun. He handed the man's revolver to them and stepped away from the site.

Okumura and Shiraiwa had taken Kiyomaru to the far end of the platform.

Ordinary passengers were starting to come up the stairs. That meant a train was arriving at the platform soon.

Mekari walked halfway down the stairs and peered into the bullet train concourse.

The riot police were baggage checking and running metal detectors over every passenger headed to the platform. It was probably less about screening people with weapons and more about frightening off anyone who didn't want to be searched.

Mekari rushed back up to the platform.

According to the electronic board, the Nozomi No. 16 bound

for Tokyo was due to pull up on Track 26 in a few minutes. If they could slip aboard the train that was about to arrive, they could depart from New Osaka without exposing Kiyomaru to the riot police. What might happen later was another matter.

It all depended on how vigilant the JR side was about Kiyomaru boarding.

About an hour had transpired since Mekari and company's arrival at the station. Thanks also to the hostage incident, the schedule was a mess.

Mekari suspected that they were beginning to lower their guard about Kiyomaru.

The Nozomi No. 16 was a Model 700 too.

Mekari, Okumura, and Shiraiwa took Kiyomaru and boarded the rearmost Car 1.

It was in the aisle between the passenger room and the operation room, the point furthest back on the car itself, that the two SPs stood with Kiyomaru. Meanwhile, Okumura sat amongst the Car 1 passengers to keep an eye out on their movements.

They'd given up on the multipurpose room this time.

To avoid exposing Kiyomaru, who'd been at the edge of the platform, they'd chosen the shortest route to get him aboard. They also didn't relish contacting the conductor, who would need to unlock the door to the room.

When the train started to move, Shiraiwa immediately checked the Kiyomaru Site. He looked sick and tired as he showed Mekari the display.

The red dot was moving away from New Osaka.

Mekari didn't feel anything anymore. This was just a condition of the transfer, he'd steeled himself.

During routine SP escorts, the VIP's schedule was public knowledge. They conducted their mission accompanied by a press horde and as the VIP's supporters and ordinary citizens assembled in huge numbers.

The only difference was whether there were many or few potential assailants, but it all came down to eliminating each threat one by one.

They would soon be arriving at Kyoto Station. From Kyoto, it was another forty minutes to Nagoya. Then, for around an hour and a half until New Yokohama, there'd be no stops. After New Yokohama it was just fifteen minutes to Tokyo Station.

Mekari felt they might somehow get it done if they could make it past Nagoya.

As long as they got by Kyoto and Nagoya.

Car 1 passengers getting off at Kyoto were guided toward the door closer to Car 2 by the conductor, who'd found out about Kiyomaru.

Mekari stepped onto the platform and looked around. Just from where he stood he could see several uniformed officers. They were boarding the train but on different cars. No one tried to come near the rearmost exit where Mekari and the others were located.

Five people had already been shot, and injured or killed, trying to attack Kiyomaru. Perhaps the mass media flashily broadcasting the fact was serving as a deterrent.

Mekari returned to the car. The exit closed and the train began to move.

The uniformed officers who'd boarded were probably Kyoto Police RPs. They were most likely patrolling the train's interior at the NPA's request.

A few minutes after departing from Kyoto Station, the automatic door to the passenger room opened and Okumura showed his face. There were two men in suits standing behind him.

"They're from the Kyoto Police Security Section. Here on orders to provide backup for the transfer team."

"We don't need any backup."

Mekari had no intention of letting people with guns get close no matter what kind of position they held.

"That's what I thought you'd say."

Okumura smiled and turned his back to Mekari and accosted the two men.

The automatic door closed.

"So it really is just the three of us from here on out…" Shiraiwa said.

"You think we should accept backup?"

"No…" Shiraiwa's face seemed to sag with weariness.

"You tired?"

"No…"

"For now, I can manage here alone. You go to the seats and take a rest."

"Mr. Mekari."

"What?"

"How does it feel to shoot someone?"

"Not bad at all."

"..."

"Much better than being shot, at least."

Shiraiwa looked at Kiyomaru, who'd sat down on the aisle floor, his back leaning against the wall, his eyes closed. It looked like he was asleep.

"I bet Mr. Sekiya would have preferred to shoot Kiyomaru if he was gonna shoot someone..."

Mekari didn't reply.

That was the end of their conversation.

With Sekiya gone, the transfer team was down to three members. Mekari didn't want to reduce their numbers any further.

Kanbashi had been shot and seriously injured. Sekiya had killed a man.

But perhaps those two were lucky. They'd at least made it out alive.

There was no telling what lied ahead. No guarantee that all three of them would survive this.

The news reporting that Kiyomaru's assailants had been injured or killed one after another had to be acting as a deterrent, but it only meant fewer people fantasizing that they could kill Kiyomaru with just a kitchen knife. Anyone still eager to go after him might use more extreme means.

Mekari was also leery of what the Ninagawa camp was up to. It was doubtful that such a meticulous outfit would settle for an unreliable method like having society at large target Kiyomaru and rest their case.

They might put pros on the job somewhere down the line, Mekari couldn't shake the feeling.

People specializing in murder.

Shortly before arriving at JR Nagoya, they received another call from Administrator Ishibashi.

At the bullet train concourse in Nagoya, officers were already checking the bags and possessions of people heading to the platform. In addition, arrangements had been made for Aichi prefecture's railway police to replace their Kyoto counterparts for the onboard patrols. All personnel had received strict orders not to approach Kiyomaru.

They arrived at Nagoya. No trouble occurred.

The hull doors shut and the train rolled out.

It felt too easy, almost weird that they'd been able to pass Kyoto and Nagoya without a hitch.

Despite himself, Mekari felt the corners of his mouth loosen a little.

When he turned to his side, Shiraiwa was also smiling again for a change.

The train suddenly came to an emergency halt. It was about half an hour past Nagoya.

What now?

They could hear a commotion from Car 1's seats.

Mekari looked outside through the exit door window. All he could see were the sky and the walls that enclosed the bullet train rails.

Kiyomaru stood up, too, and gazed through the window on the opposite side.

Mekari drew his SIG and opened the automatic door to the seats. Okumura came running.

"Someone's been taken hostage. The perp demands we bring Kiyomaru."

Apparently a boy around high school age had drawn a large survival knife and was holding it to a sales trolley girl.

"Again?!" Shiraiwa spat.

"Mr. Okumura, what should we do? Mind being the one to shoot and kill someone this time?" Mekari asked gently.

Okumura sagged and shook his head.

Mekari opened the metal plate on the wall next to the outside door and pulled the emergency handle.

Shiraiwa opened and jumped out the door, drew his SIG, and scanned the area.

Mekari unloaded Kiyomaru before dropping down onto the tracks himself. Okumura followed behind him.

No one else exited the train.

Mekari, Okumura, and Shiraiwa took Kiyomaru and began to walk along the tracks. They were bound to come to an entry-way for track maintenance.

What might happen now was anyone's guess, but they'd at least be able to get rid of their Public Security tail. They could continue their transfer without their whereabouts being known.

Mekari had no desire whatsoever to contact the higher-ups. He had a thought.

We've declared independence from the Japanese police

organization.

They were a team of just three.

They couldn't trust anyone else.

2

The trees and shrubs were thick. The branches that reached out from both sides formed a green ceiling.

Since a while back, they could hear the thrumming of a helicopter. They couldn't tell if it was the police or the media, but there was little worry of them being spotted from above.

Mekari and company had been walking this path for almost thirty minutes. It wasn't exactly a mountain trail. These were just hills.

They'd yet to see a single person or car since leaving the train.

There wasn't any signal for their phones so it was impossible to check the Kiyomaru Site, but they'd no doubt ditched their Public Security tail. Anyone trying to follow them here had to be an idiot.

Mekari had no clue where "here" was. Given that they'd gotten off the train about thirty minutes after Nagoya, they probably hadn't crossed into Shizuoka prefecture yet. They were likely somewhere in Aichi.

They had no choice but to keep taking the trail downward.

It was now past five in the afternoon. The sooner they came out to somewhere where they could get a car, the better.

Mekari wanted to secure their next mode of transportation

before the sun set.

"How much are you planning on making me walk?!" Kiyomaru moaned, sitting down on the wayside. "I'll wait here, so you guys go find and bring back a car."

This shit, who the fuck does he think he is?

Mekari stepped forward, meaning to punch Kiyomaru.

"Try again, you bastard!"

Shiraiwa acted first and kicked the suspect. Before he could get in a second hit, Kiyomaru quickly stood up and began walking. Just then, they heard the sound of a car.

When they turned around, they saw a worn-out light truck headed their way. Shiraiwa spread his arms and stopped it.

"What you folks doin' there?" a voice called from the driver's seat. It was an old man who looked to be in his seventies.

Okumura walked closer. "I apologize for making such a request, but could you possibly take us to a street where we could grab a taxi?"

"Can only fit one next to me, but if the rest of you don't mind sitting in the back."

A small amount of timber was stacked on the bed. Okumura took the passenger seat, and the truck began to move with the other three in the back.

The wind felt good against Mekari's sweaty body. The last time he'd been rocked on the bed of a truck was way back in grade school, when his uncle had let him ride behind him on a three-wheeler.

It was the first pleasant transit of the day.

After fifteen minutes or so, the truck stopped at what looked like a national route. Mekari and Shiraiwa jumped off the back, and Kiyomaru followed.

Okumura stepped down from the passenger side and took a few bills from his wallet. He said to the aged driver, "You really helped us out. This isn't much, but please, as a token of appreciation." He held out the bills.

"I ain't a taxi…" The old man pushed Okumura's hand away. "Gotta accept people's kindness graciously. See someone in trouble, show them kindness. As your thanks to me…"

He gave them a wrinkly smile and drove off.

Mekari, Okumura, Shiraiwa, and even Kiyomaru stared after the retreating truck in silence.

If the old man had known that Kiyomaru was with them, would he have been waylaid by the one billion too?

No, probably not.

The elderly driver hadn't looked well-off by a long shot, but he seemed quite content with his life.

If you were satisfied with your modest happiness, you wouldn't be tempted by a load of cash.

Was the world nowadays filled with too many people who had yet to taste satisfaction?

The light truck had already disappeared from view.

It took around ten minutes, but they were able to hail a cab.

"Please take us to the closest car rental store," Okumura said as he got on the passenger side.

The news was playing through the car radio. It was reporting on the Nozomi No. 16 hostage situation. It appeared that the deadlock was continuing.

The railway police who were on board could handle it. Mekari decided to leave it at that.

The news then began to touch on the side effects of Kiyomaru's transfer.

Apparently people mistaken for him had been attacked all over the country and been injured or killed. Just the fatalities already numbered six cases. The timing of each of the incidents lagged well behind Kiyomaru's actual transfer. Probably not everyone hoping to kill him for the one billion was checking the Kiyomaru Site.

Mekari couldn't believe that some people would go ahead and murder the wrong person in the absence of precise info.

It was nuts. He was drawn back into a gloomy mood.

They got off the taxi after around twenty minutes. There was a family restaurant next to the car rental store. Now that Mekari thought about it, they hadn't eaten since breakfast. It was time they stopped for a meal.

Shiraiwa was sent to rent a car by himself, while Mekari, Okumura, and Kiyomaru entered the family restaurant.

They were shown to a table in the back. The restaurant was about four tenths full.

A waitress came to take their order. Kiyomaru ordered an Italian hamburger set, and Okumura Chinese noodles. Mekari ordered a BLT sandwich for himself and curry rice for Shiraiwa.

A large flat-screen monitor was mounted on the wall. The

sound had been turned off, but the afternoon news program was recapping how the transfer had gone so far today.

A video displayed the convoy as it traveled along the highway. They'd even captured the semi-trailer that had broken through the blockade and rammed into the patrol car. Moreover, what followed was the blood-soaked aisle on the Nozomi No. 86.

Looking at those images, Mekari felt as though they had nothing to do with him.

When he saw the pool of blood on the platform at New Osaka, however, his heart sank a bit.

They showed the perp. It appeared they were using a photo from when he was ten years younger. With plenty of hair on his head, he was laughing in a double-buttoned suit. His face brimmed with confidence.

"Did you already order?"

Having entered the restaurant in the meantime, Shiraiwa placed the car keys on the table. He sat next to Mekari.

"Yeah, I ordered for you too."

"Huh, what did you order?"

Just then, Mekari noticed a young couple seated a little ways from them stretching up and glancing around. Almost as though they were looking for someone.

He had a bad feeling.

He pulled out his cell phone. He had three bars of signal. He accessed the Kiyomaru Site.

His screen showed the map.

Mekari felt his blood freeze.

Shiraiwa peered into the screen. The blinking red dot was

stopped at a family restaurant along a national route. There was a car rental store next to it, and a label: Toyohashi City, Aichi Prefecture.

Their precise location.

"They found us?" Okumura guessed just from observing Mekari and Shiraiwa.

Mekari looked around the establishment. It appeared that multiple groups of guests had already noticed.

They didn't know since when, but faces also lined the windows, peering in.

Mekari drew his SIG and gripped it under the table.

How?!

Hadn't they shaken off Public Security? Neither that old man nor the taxi driver could know that they'd entered the family restaurant.

Customers started entering one after the other. They ignored the waitress who came to seat them and simply glanced around.

The team needed to get a move on right away. Mekari whispered into Shiraiwa's ear, "Bring the car out of the lot and right to the front."

Shiraiwa ran out without uttering a word.

Mekari had a sudden thought.

Is it Shiraiwa?

If Shiraiwa had contacted someone while at the car rental…

In the end, it was doubtful they were still being tailed. That meant that there was a traitor amongst the transfer team.

Okumura reached into his wallet and placed a five-thousand-yen note on the table.

Kiyomaru looked pale.

Mekari hid the SIG under his jacket and stood up. He and Okumura sandwiched Kiyomaru between them and headed towards the exit.

The customers' eyes were all on Kiyomaru. But to Mekari, none of them looked like anything more than blatantly curious spectators.

A gang of smirking youths blocked the exit. Mekari pointed his gun at them.

"You wouldn't dare," one of them said.

Pointing the gun upwards, Mekari fired a shot.

A tremendous blast echoed. Somewhere in the back, a woman screamed.

The youths immediately scrambled out of sight.

Shiraiwa had parked a white four-door sedan by the front exit. With the passenger and back seat doors opened, he was waiting SIG in hand.

Mekari continued to intimidate the onlookers with his SIG as they got into the car.

Okumura got into the passenger seat, Kiyomaru and Mekari in the back.

Shiraiwa zoomed off.

But where to?

3

The blinking red dot was moving along National Route 1 towards

Shizuoka prefecture. Mekari ended the i-mode and put away his phone.

"Where should we go from here?" Shiraiwa, who gripped the wheel, asked him.

So far, the road was pretty empty. No cars seemed to be following them. But as they went on, they'd be surrounded by vehicles sooner or later. In addition to assailants, onlookers would no doubt gather en masse.

It wasn't the kind of scenario they could escape with a car chase. They needed to stop somewhere while they still had the chance and regroup, but it was difficult to say where.

Crowded spots heightened the risk of an attack and bringing harm to innocent citizens. Yet burrowing into somewhere inaccessible could very well spell the end of the transfer. For instance, if they locked themselves into a hotel room then no one could reach Kiyomaru in there, but the hallway would soon be flooded with people and they wouldn't be able to leave.

They'd have to bring in the riot police, and that would be the most dangerous moment.

Either way, Mekari wanted to stop. But they couldn't let themselves be trapped while they were parked.

"Are there any clearings nearby? Somewhere with lots of potential exits…"

He didn't have a concrete image of the kind of place he wanted-ed.

Shiraiwa and Okumura consulted the navigation system that came with the rental car. Scrolling, they inspected their surroundings.

The sight of the car navigation screen almost made Mekari feel like he was looking at the Kiyomaru Site.

His heart started beating faster.

GPS.

A car navigation system used GPS, which pinpointed locations via data from a geostationary satellite. Perhaps their whereabouts had been tracked accurately throughout the transfer not because of a Public Security tail, but thanks to GPS.

All police cars were equipped with devices called a car locator. It allowed dispatched police cars to be tracked and displayed in real time in the comms room via GPS.

Weren't they being tracked in the same way? The Ninagawa camp, obtaining info via GPS and streaming it onto their site through an advanced display system...

Come to think of it, Mekari had recently seen a TV commercial for cell phones equipped with GPS. He hadn't had the slightest interest at the time, but if someone with a GPS-equipped cell phone was close to Kiyomaru, that was all it'd take to relay precise locational data to the Ninagawa camp on an ongoing basis.

Kiyomaru had received a full body check prior to the transfer and wasn't carrying anything. He couldn't possibly have been handed something without him noticing, either.

The same went for Mekari.

Suddenly he felt all the blood rush to his head.

He'd been betrayed from the start. By Shiraiwa, or Okumura.

Shiraiwa's cell phone looked like a newer model. Was it equipped with GPS? Even if it wasn't, it wouldn't be strange for him to have a second phone.

Mekari couldn't remember seeing Okumura use a cell phone, but it was certainly plausible that he had a GPS-loaded device of some sort in his pockets.

Doubting Shiraiwa didn't sit well with Mekari, but he couldn't deny the possibility. Nor did Okumura seem like such a underhanded man. Yet one of them had to be connected to the Ninagawa camp.

Perhaps Shiraiwa had spouted that stuff early on about a billion yen gained through murder not buying happiness just to gain Mekari's trust.

Had Okumura brought up that bit about a Public Security tail to keep suspicions from turning inward on the team?

Mekari's head felt like a whirlpool of rage and doubt, ready to burst.

"What about there?" Okumura offered.

In front of them and to the left was a large, empty plot of land. It looked like it could hold two baseball stadiums with ease. If this was the planned site of a large-scale public project, all that had been done so far was to level the area. There was nothing enclosing it, not even barbed wire.

"Good, let's stop here."

Following Mekari's approval, Shiraiwa drove the car into the empty lot.

They parked in the center of the vast field of red dirt. All four sides appeared to have roads running along them.

Here, they could glimpse any approaching cars from a good distance, and they had numerous escape routes.

Mekari invited Shiraiwa and Okumura and got out from the

car. The two left the vehicle and approached Mekari. They left the engine on.

Kiyomaru watched the three men from the open door to the rear seat.

"I just wanted to check something here," Mekari said, strangling his emotions and feigning calm.

"What's wrong? Check what?" Shiraiwa responded irritatedly.

Mekari's anger and doubt must have been evident despite his best efforts. "The belongings we have on our persons," he said.

"You mean for us to give each other body checks?" rephrased Okumura, as coolly as ever.

"That's right."

"Are you saying you doubt me too?" asked Shiraiwa, looking unsettled.

"I just want to get rid of all possibilities, one at a time. If you've got nothing to hide, there's no reason to refuse."

"Why do I have to be doubted though?!"

"Why are you getting so worked up?"

"Because you're doubting me!"

"Then tell me why our location's been an open book to the enemy."

"That's…"

"The only possible answer is that one of us three is connected to Ninagawa."

"Well, is it you, then?!" yelled Shiraiwa. "I already know it's not me! That means the traitor's one of you!"

Shiraiwa was at a breaking point.

Mekari stared into his junior partner's eyes and tried to make sense of the reaction. Was he panicking because his betrayal was coming to light, or was he pissed that a guy with whom he thought he enjoyed mutual trust was doubting him? Mekari couldn't decide.

"Well then, why don't we start by body checking you, Mekari, since you started this," proposed Okumura.

"Yeah, that's right! Take out everything you've got on you!" Shiraiwa advanced on Mekari.

"Stop!" Kiyomaru yelled. He got out of the car and ran towards Mekari. "I might get shot while they're body checking you!"

Shiraiwa looked at Kiyomaru in disbelief. "Him, you trust?"

"At least more than you guys… When I almost got shot, he's the only one who shielded me."

"You fucking shit!" Shiraiwa drew his SIG and pointed it at Kiyomaru. A vein was pulsing in the SP's brow. "Who do you think I've been risking my life for?!"

Mekari had drawn his SIG almost simultaneously. "Shiraiwa! Lower your gun!" His own was aimed at his colleague.

"What? You pull a gun on *me*?!" Shiraiwa glared at Mekari with terrifying eyes. "Are you telling me you value Kiyomaru's life over mine?!"

Mekari didn't want to shoot Shiraiwa but was mad as hell.

Either Shiraiwa or Okumura was the traitor. Why *wouldn't* he find the traitor less forgivable than Kiyomaru?

Mekari looked at Okumura, who was calmly lighting a cigarette, and said, "Mr. Okumura, what have you got to say?"

"I agree with Shiraiwa," an earnest reply came. "Beats me why anyone would value Kiyomaru's life over his buddy's."

Buddy? Who? One of us three has to be the enemy!

"I don't give a shit about the money! I'll kill Kiyomaru so we can end this goddamn mission!" Shiraiwa screamed.

Mekari stood in front of Shiraiwa's gun. Kiyomaru hid behind Mekari.

"Shiraiwa, drop the gun." Still aiming at him, Mekari slowly moved closer.

"You're in the way!" Shiraiwa bellowed.

I should have recognized the signs sooner.

Shiraiwa had gone and cracked.

"Because Kiyomaru's alive, countless people have died. We should just kill off scum like him!"

Mekari stopped moving. The two SIGs crossed each other.

"You won't be able to kill Kiyomaru without killing me first," Mekari said staring into Shiraiwa's eyes. "But if you kill me and kill Kiyomaru, you'll be sentenced to death."

"Mr. Mekari." Tears started to spill from both of Shiraiwa's eyes. "Mr. Mekari…"

Mekari suddenly felt unsure.

"Mr. Mekari, why…" Shiraiwa was looking straight back at him. "If you can't believe me, what *will* you believe?!"

A stabbing pain tormented Mekari as though a needle had been thrust through his heart.

"Hey!"

At Okumura's voice, Mekari and Shiraiwa turned around at the same time.

A car was approaching from the distance. It looked like a high-roofed four wheel drive. A man was leaning out from the passenger's seat with a long-barreled firearm.

"It's a shotgun!" Mekari shouted.

Okumura had already dashed to the driver's seat. Shiraiwa dove in from the other side. Mekari shoved Kiyomaru into the back and followed right in. They took off before he could even close the door.

But two cars were approaching from the opposite direction as well.

Whether the three vehicles were working together or trying to get the jump on one another was hard to say.

A dry report rang out. The door mirror on the passenger side blew off.

The shotgun—a powerful firearm used by hunters that could shoot anywhere from several to several hundred lead pellets. The most popular 12 Gauge model, loaded with 00 buck for hunting deer, could fire nine pieces of lead that were each comparable to .380 ACP ammo. 12 Gauge Buckshot was said to be your best bet should a lion charge you.

Being targeted with such a weapon was something else. Mekari and Kiyomaru had their heads ducked low. Okumura sped up.

The station wagon to their front came ramming in.

Okumura veered the handle left. Almost brushing the sedan rapidly closing in from behind, he steered further left.

They ended up facing the 4WD that was giving them chase. A gunshot rang out.

Red dirt exploded right by their car.

Okumura turned the wheel again to try to slip through, but the station wagon that had rushed in was blocking their way.

Okumura stomped on the break. There was a slight impact.

They'd come into contact with the flank of the station wagon and stopped. The sedan was nearing behind them.

The man in the 4WD's shotgun seat fired the namesake weapon. A gunshot rang out again, and red dirt danced into the air even closer by.

The shotgun appeared to be aimed at their tires. The plan seemed to be to render their car immobile before attacking Kiyomaru.

The man with the shotgun who'd been leaning out the window retreated back inside. He was probably reloading.

The 4WD was fast approaching.

"Fuck this!"

In a rage, Shiraiwa leapt out of their car and let his SIG loose at the 4WD.

Plumes rose all around it. At the sixth shot, a tire blew.

Even slowed to a crawl, the 4WD continued to approach.

The shotgunner leaned out of the window again, his weapon at the ready. Shiraiwa pointed the muzzle of his SIG at him.

Two gun shots rang out at the same time.

The top half of Shiraiwa's head blew off.

4

Shiraiwa's body lay on the red dirt.

His head looked like a popped pomegranate. There wasn't much of anything left you'd call a head.

Mekari felt his blood churn. The hair on his head stood on end.

He thrust his SIG in front of Kiyomaru's face and fired rapidly through the window.

Every time a bullet made contact with the windshield of the approaching 4WD, the more it misted.

The vehicle swerved wildly and showed its flank to Mekari.

He continued to pull the trigger. He funneled as many bullets as he could into the 4WD's shotgun seat.

Burnt empty casings were raining down on Kiyomaru.

More and more dark holes appeared along the 4WD's passenger side. Blood visibly sprayed out of the window. The shotgun dropped to the ground.

Mekari's SIG ran out of ammo, and the slide retreated and stopped. Discarding the empty magazine, he drew a spare from the pouch at his waist and slammed it into the SIG. He raised the slide stop and sent the first bullet into the chamber.

The 4WD was turning to flee. The station wagon blocking their front started running as well.

Cracks splintered across the station wagon's windshield from two bullet holes.

Okumura had shot his New Nambu at it.

Now he stepped on the accelerator. The car sped forward.

The sedan behind wasn't coming after them, either.

Okumura tossed the revolver in his right hand into the passenger's seat and focused on driving. They skidded out of the empty lot and zipped down the road.

A considerable number of cars had gathered around the empty lot. Mekari stuck his SIG out from the window on his side as a warning but none moved to approach, perhaps cowered by the earlier gunshots.

Kiyomaru was crouched with his hands over both ears. Mekari also felt acute pain in his ears.

It was rapidly growing dark.

Mekari pulled out his cell phone so Okumura wouldn't notice and checked the Kiyomaru Site.

The red dot had already entered Shizuoka. It was moving along Route 42 towards Hamana Lake.

He quickly ended the i-mode and put away his phone.

"Mr. Okumura, could we stop somewhere for a second?"

His own voice sounded faraway.

Okumura nodded.

After driving for a while more, they pulled up at an abandoned gasoline station. Okumura turned the car so they were facing the road and parked.

Mekari thrust his SIG against the back of Okumura's head.

"Shiraiwa's dead. There's no one else left."

He was surprised at how cold his own voice sounded.

The detective took his time turning around. He looked at Mekari, coolly.

"Get out," Mekari said, poking Okumura's head with the barrel of his SIG.

Okumura showed no fear as he opened the door and slowly stepped onto the ground.

Mekari scrambled out of the car and circled around, his SIG pointed at Okumura all along the way.

He stopped about two meters in front of the man.

"How did you relay our position? Was it with a GPS-equipped cell?"

"Yup." Okumura pulled one out of his jacket pocket. "All I did was have this in my pocket. You see, a satellite kept track of us this whole time," he said with a faint grin.

"Why don't you hand that to me."

"If I say I don't want to, are you gonna shoot me?"

"I will."

"You'd kill me to protect Kiyomaru?"

"Kill you, no. I'm just gonna try to shoot the phone. I'm not sure I'll hit it, though…"

"A grand violation of our police code."

"I don't care how much questioning I have to deal with afterwards."

"All right."

Okumura tossed the phone in his hand, and it tumbled to Mekari's feet.

Mekari blasted it with his SIG.

The gunshot echoed, and shards scattered. It was obvious at a glance that it had been completely destroyed.

The satellite's lost us for good now.

"Are you satisfied?" Okumura said as though he could read Mekari's thoughts.

Mekari opened his mouth and let out a question he needed to ask. "Why did you act as an accomplice to this stupid business?"

"Here's the thing, as long as I continued to let them know where we were, regardless of who killed Kiyomaru, I would also get a billion."

"…"

"I have no intention of serving time at my age. Getting a billion without ever being arrested. No one else in Japan has my sweet deal."

"Don't you have any pride as a detective?"

"I do. Been with the force for over thirty years. I think I have a decent amount of pride and a sense of justice," intoned Okumura. "But I'm close to retiring age. And it's not like I've enough saved to spend my retirement in leisure…"

"You're an accomplice to murder! You smeared filth all over your past thirty years in the force!"

"And what would you know about that?" A cold light entered Okumura's eyes. "You know, I saw Chika Ninagawa's corpse…"

Mekari's breath caught.

"What can someone who's only seen the case in the news know?"

Okumura's expression had changed. He looked even more enraged than Mekari.

"The horror of that site, how painful that child's body looked… It's far beyond anything you could imagine."

Mekari couldn't respond.

"It's not like the police lets everything out to the mass media. There are things the news can broadcast and things they mustn't. There are plenty of things we hold back out of consideration for the grieving family."

Okumura looked towards Kiyomaru.

The window glass on Kiyomaru's side had been shattered by Mekari's gunfire so he could probably hear their voices, but hidden in the darkness of the back seat his face was invisible.

"That guy snapped both ankles on a seven year old before brutally raping her. Then he pummeled her until she was dead. The kid's face looked like an overripe persimmon, red and leaking…"

Okumura's voice choked.

"The girl's face was so swollen the doctor couldn't even pry her eyelids open, and that guy had shot semen all over it! Could you?! Tell her parents that, too?!"

He was shedding tears. Despite always seeming so calm, Okumura could no longer check his emotions.

Mekari realized his own folly.

He'd thought of Okumura and Kanbashi as fellow cops on the same transfer team, but he'd been mistaken.

Between himself and men who'd stood at the site and faced the victim's body, who'd breathed the family's grief and anger and searched for the culprit, perceptions of Kiyomaru were as distant as heaven and earth.

It sank into Mekari far too late that Kanbashi's roughness towards Kiyomaru hadn't merely been a character issue.

"They knew who the culprit was immediately. The DNA matched. We searched desperately for Kiyomaru. We ran around day after endless day. Yet, no hint of him. After three months, there isn't much more you can do. A resigned mood set in at special investigation HQ. But I couldn't forgive Kiyomaru. I wanted to make him pay for it, no matter what. That's when that man appeared…"

Okumura was no longer shedding any tears, and he'd returned to his usual calm way of speaking.

"He said he worked for the victim's family, so I met with him. I felt guilty because we weren't any closer to arresting Kiyomaru… He was a very strange man. But he was the one who'd been hired by old Ninagawa to actually take charge of this insane affair. I could tell right away that he was no ordinary fellow. Not normal. As proof, he spoke to me long before the transfer team was put together. Which means he has influence over MPD brass at the very least."

"…"

"Even with old Ninagawa's pull, you can't get higher-ups to become accomplices to crime. My guess is that the man's moved in intelligence circles. A professional schemer. He was quite adept at using the carrot and the stick. Those who don't fall to bribes he coerces by getting the dirt on them. Before I knew it, I'd agreed, too…"

"What sort of dirt did he get on you?"

"Why should I tell?" Okumura said, his expression not even flickering. "So, what's your plan now? Are you going to arrest me?"

"I'll have the local police do it."

Okumura snorted at Mekari's words. "Wonder whom the local police will believe? There's no proof that I've been hired by Ninagawa."

"There's a witness!" Kiyomaru yelled, sticking his head out of the back seat window.

"If you're still alive…" Okumura said coldly. "You're hoping to go to the police and testify? They'll blow your head off before your rear can hit the chair."

Kiyomaru froze.

Okumura turned around to face Mekari again.

"If Kiyomaru dies, it's just your word against mine. Exposing my crime means exposing some MPD boss, I don't know who. Do you really think you can do that without evidence?"

It was exactly as Okumura said. Not a chance.

"I want you to think about this rationally. You're a fine police officer. I think you're an excellent SP. And a standup human being, too. Is Kiyomaru worth someone like you risking his life? Nope. Not one bit!"

Okumura's delivery was getting heated again.

"I didn't try to get Kiyomaru killed by someone just because I was hired by Ninagawa. If, after meeting Kiyomaru, I could find even a smidgeon of a reason to allow him to live, I meant to toss that phone away and give protecting him my all."

Mekari couldn't sense any lie in Okumura's words.

"But that man's nothing but scum! Letting him live is what makes you complicit with evil! Say we protect him to the end—he's handed his sentence in court, taxpayers keep him fed behind bars for ten years or so, and when he gets out, he'll kill another girl soon enough. Am I wrong? When that happens, what words of apology will you have for the murdered girl?!"

Mekari couldn't reply. He feared things would turn out exactly as Okumura said.

"See? Time to call it quits. Ninagawa's serious. He won't give up. I don't know what other plans he may have made for the future. The one who'll be in danger then is you. I don't want you to die!"

"…"

"Even if you deliver Kiyomaru to the MPD, he'll get killed somewhere down the line. In detention, the prosecutor's office, jail, court, prison… And during that time, more people will be mistaken for Kiyomaru and killed, bystanders getting caught in the fray. All of Japan's feeling murderous. And it'll continue until Kiyomaru dies."

Okumura spoke true.

"Let's just end this. Or else there'll definitely come a time when you'll regret letting Kiyomaru live. I'll shoot the guy. We'll say he lost hope and stole my gun and committed suicide. You get half my reward money. Half a billion. Go on as a cop like you've nothing to answer for, or retire early in luxury."

There was fear on Kiyomaru's face. It was the first time he looked completely bereft of hope.

Mekari replied, "Mr. Okumura, I hear you. But I can't accept your invitation."

He placed both of Okumura's hands on the car's hood and patted him down.

"No other cell phone?"

"Nope, I never took to them…"

He didn't have anything else suspicious on his person. Mekari took Okumura's handcuffs along with the key.

Mekari opened the door to the back seat and snapped the

handcuffs on Kiyomaru's wrists.

Then he got in the driver's seat and started the engine. He noticed the New Nambu on the shotgun seat and took it in hand.

When he opened the cylinder and pointed the gun upwards, three unused .38 special bullets slipped out and rolled onto the floor. The two empty casings were burned in and didn't fall.

He tossed the New Nambu at Okumura's feet. It made a loud metallic clang against the concrete ground.

"This is your last chance to reconsider. You'll come to regret this," Okumura said.

"You're probably right…" answered Mekari.

"Then why?"

"Shiraiwa died. I can't kill Kiyomaru and take the money now."

"Nothing good'll come of serving the dead."

"I know that!" Mekari snarled. He stepped forcefully on the accelerator.

He left Okumura at the abandoned gasoline station and drove the car back onto the road.

Nothing good'll come of serving the dead.

Okumura's words rang in his ears.

He knew that already.

Subsection Chief Ohki had once said something similar to him.

I know that. But I don't know how else to live.

Shiraiwa was dead.

He'd allowed Shiraiwa to die.

He'd thought Shiraiwa had cracked. But he was wrong.

Mekari was the one who'd come apart, a long time ago. Possessed by anger and doubt, he'd been unable to make a sound decision.

It was Shiraiwa whom he should have believed to the end.

Kiyomaru leaned forward from the back seat. "I knew it, you're just the man I thought! You're the only one I can trust!"

Mekari felt the same way. Ironically, the only person he could call his ally now was human scum that went by the name of Kiyomaru.

And the fact was exceedingly unpleasant.

Chapter 5

One Person

1

Night had fully fallen.

The car carrying Mekari and Kiyomaru sped on the Hamana Bypass. Putting the Araibenten IC behind them, they crossed the Great Hamana Bridge.

Shiraiwa's figure and Okumura's words spiraled in Mekari's head.

The sight of Shiraiwa's head blowing apart had been burned into his memory.

He could hear Okumura's tearful voice.

Like an overripe persimmon... shot semen all over...

Shiraiwa's smiling face resurfaced.

He felt like he was going mad.

The Hamana Bypass had merged with National Route 1. They stopped at a red light.

Mekari snapped back to himself and checked the time. Over ten minutes had passed since he'd abandoned Okumura and begun driving.

He needed to ditch this car soon. The door mirror on one side was missing, and the window was shattered. There were several bullet holes in the frame as well. Okumura knew about it, and many others had witnessed its state.

Okumura had been deprived of his cell phone and left at a place with minimal traffic. It would take some time for him to contact the Ninagawa camp.

There were two things Mekari had to do before then. First, to get as far away as possible from Okumura, and second, to contact his superior.

The light turned to green. Mekari stepped on the accelerator.

He took out his cell phone. After some thought, he called Subsection Chief Ohki.

"Mekari?! Where are you now?! What happened to Kiyomaru?!" Ohki's excited voice pounded on his ear.

"Kiyomaru is safe. Shiraiwa, however, died."

"…"

"Please contact the Shizuoka Police and tell them to detain Assistant Inspector Okumura. That man works for Ninagawa."

"What did you say?!"

"Okumura was hired by Ninagawa and was letting them know where we were. He admitted it himself. The Metropolitan Police brass are also involved."

"Is that really true?!"

"Kiyomaru is my witness."

Ohki fell silent. He wasn't responding.

"Is something the matter, Subsection Chief?"

"We've…actually received a report from Assistant Inspector Okumura."

"Huh?"

"He said that Kiyomaru saw the chance to steal a gun, took

you hostage, and is on the run..."

"What?!"

"We were told that Kiyomaru is feeling cornered and desperate and that your life is in peril."

"..."

"Upon receiving that report, the Metropolitan Police immediately sent out a directive. Rescuing Assistant Inspector Mekari, who's been taken hostage, is our top priority. As soon as they're spotted, Kiyomaru is to be shot on sight..."

Yikes...

Mekari had underestimated Ninagawa.

A permission slip to shoot Kiyomaru had been handed to all police.

They'd anticipated Okumura getting kicked out of the transfer team and scripted a plan.

But how had Okumura informed them so soon? Did there just happen to be a toll phone near that abandoned gasoline station?

No, Ninagawa's men had probably been pursuing them to support Okumura. Multiple teams, at that. They must have followed Mekari's team at a distance with orders to pick up Okumura as soon as the GPS signal went out.

"The Shizuoka Police have sent everyone they can spare to search for you. Riot police from adjacent prefectures are also going to assemble at the borders to monitor them."

They'd reacted far too quickly. They had to be operating according to a pre-made scenario. Mekari couldn't help but think that the man hired by Ninagawa to manage everything was enjoying some massive game.

"Mekari, how can I help? Should I send backup, our own people from Security Sec?"

"No. Right now, I'm unable to trust anyone who comes near."

"Isn't there, isn't there anything I can do?"

"Pray for us. For me and Kiyomaru…"

Mekari hung up.

They heard police sirens with unnatural frequency. Patrol cars were crisscrossing the whole town.

They'd ditched the car shortly after his call to Ohki. If they were pulled over for an inspection, that would be the end of it.

Instead of leaving it along the road, Mekari had snuck it away in a coin parking lot. The longer the police took to find it, the better.

Two hours had passed since then.

A full wide-range deployment covering the entirety of Shizuoka prefecture had to be in effect, with no gaps even for an ant to crawl out undetected.

Mobilizing the maximum number of personnel on alert from all of the prefecture's precincts, they were conducting inspections at checkpoints on the main roads, train stations, and ports, and in the meantime searching every nook and cranny where they might be hiding.

They'd eventually be found, Kiyomaru would be shot to death, and, for sure, Mekari alongside him.

If a police squad spotted them, some officer enthused by the one-billion-yen prey was more likely than not to open fire without warning. His buddies would no doubt also let loose. As long as they got off a shot, regardless of whose bullet made the kill they'd have a claim on the billion.

Mekari remembered the TV program at the cafeteria from the day before last. Specifically, the conditions for obtaining the billion-yen reward listed on the Kiyomaru Site:

1. To receive a guilty verdict for a murder or manslaughter charge against Kunihide Kiyomaru (multiple persons possible).

2. To be publicly recognized as being responsible for the death of Kunihide Kiyomaru (multiple persons possible).

Mekari belatedly understood the kind of case Condition Two indicated.

The current situation. Causing lethal injury to Kiyomaru in the line of duty.

The Ninagawa camp must have had the scenario in mind from the beginning when they drafted those rules.

Mekari wondered what Subsection Chief Ohki had done after the call. Was he capable of turning the tide of events? Sadly no, not by far. The likely outcome was that the call itself would get squashed. There were people connected with Ninagawa in the upper stratum of the MPD, and the NPA too. If someone claimed that Mekari had spoken under duress, threatened by a gun-toting Kiyomaru, that would be the end of it.

They were in an unmanned roadside police box in the suburbs of Hamamatsu.

A man who was being hunted by the entire prefectural police couldn't possibly be holed up in a police box. At a time when all personnel had been mobilized—even the ones off-duty called up with a "dorm summons" and posted across the prefecture—no officer would drop by an unmanned police box in the burbs.

Mekari was pretty sure.

He was tired. He was hungry.

Exhaustion and hunger sapped your will.

"You must be hungry, I'll go buy some food at a convenience store," Mekari said. He'd noted one close by on their way.

"No, I'm good. I'm not hungry."

Fear was written all over Kiyomaru's face. He was afraid that Mekari might go shopping and never come back.

As long as Mekari acted alone, there was no risk. The local police wouldn't know what he looked like.

Yet Kiyomaru was terrified of being left on his own. It was only natural. If Mekari gave up on him, all that awaited was death. His situation was hopeless.

Even if they managed to stay hidden in the police box until the emergency deployment was lifted, there was nowhere to go. If they could slip out of Shizuoka, they might get by after that. But they lacked the means.

They might somehow find a car or board a long-distance bus, but they wouldn't make it past any checkpoint. Were they supposed to smuggle themselves out on a freight truck like in some old movie? It was doubtful they could clear inspections that way.

As for stations and ports, they dared not even tiptoe close.

Should they cross the mountains on foot, then? The borders of Shizuoka, Nagano, and Yamanashi prefectures were mountainous. The police didn't have enough boots to cover all that terrain.

By taking to the mountains, they might be able to climb over the border without being seen by police.

But Mekari was no mountaineer. He also had no clue about the region's geography. He didn't even know how tall the peaks were or how many dozens or hundreds of kilometers of a hike it would be.

Taking to the mountains was like going to their deaths.

Should he contact the media and try to disclose the truth? Pointless. Who would believe him without proof?

Should he seek help from someone he could trust? But there was no one he could trust. If he did, he wasn't involving anyone so dear to him.

"It's over. I'm as good as dead..." mumbled Kiyomaru.

Mekari didn't say anything. *That's not true, don't give up*—the words would've only sounded hollow.

"It's not that I'm scared of dying. I mean, if I have to live like this, why not just croak already, right?"

Mekari didn't have any words for Kiyomaru.

"But you know, I just can't stand being slaughtered by the sort of people who're blinded by a billion yen."

Kiyomaru means to kill himself.

Mekari was only half right, however, and half wrong.

Kiyomaru stared straight at him.

"Kill me."

Mekari thought he'd misheard.

"If it's at your hand, I'll happily go on to the other side." Kiyomaru's eyes were serious. "Like in self-defense? They're already pretending that I've taken you hostage. When I tried to kill you,

you fought back and killed me instead. You'd get off scot-free."

"…"

"Then the one billion will be yours. Just a little is fine, so could you send some money to my mom?"

Kiyomaru's mother lived in Hokkaido. Mekari had heard that it'd been just the two of them from back when Kiyomaru was born.

"I haven't done a single thing to show my thanks to her until now. I mean, I've only brought shame to her…"

The son she'd raised singlehandedly had raped and murdered a young girl. After getting out of prison, he'd killed again, unrepentant. It wasn't hard to imagine how tough her life had been.

Being his mother, she was in her fifties or thereabouts. She was another victim of Kiyomaru's, no mistake.

"In exchange for her son's life at least, give her enough money to support her in her old age."

Kiyomaru, too, was someone's child. Mekari pitied him for not wising up until it had come to this.

"Are you really sure you can trust me that much?" Mekari asked him. "I might just take all the money for myself. You said when we first met that you didn't trust anyone other than yourself…"

"No, I can trust you. More than myself…"

Kiyomaru kept looking straight at Mekari.

Sly bastard.

No, perhaps Kiyomaru didn't have an ulterior motive. But after hearing those words, Mekari couldn't let him die.

Is this what Ninagawa—or rather, the man he hired to oversee this crazy game—aimed for?

If the goal were to kill Kiyomaru, then professional assassins or a squad of mercenaries would have sufficed.

The main purpose of the bounty must have been to scare Kiyomaru out of hiding. But what followed hinted at a motive beyond just killing him.

Hunted by all of Japan, with even the police force devolving into a murderous outfit, he would feel cornered, have nowhere to turn, taste despair.

Was it out of consideration for Ninagawa, who might not be satisfied with simply murdering a culprit who seemed immune to remorse? Was it to drive home to Kiyomaru the grief and anger that his crime had wrought—on the far shore of his own fear and despair?

Was the formation of a transfer team that included SPs, and Mekari's selection as one of its members, and his being with Kiyomaru now, perhaps all part of a scenario that the man had laid out in advance?

That wasn't actually possible. No one could have predicted how Mekari, tasked with the mission, would feel, think, and act. Yet, he couldn't shake the idea that he was merely fulfilling a role he'd been assigned, in a narrative concocted by some nameless figure.

And that was making his gut boil with rage.

Cut the fuck out! Enough is enough!

He wasn't letting them play this shitty game forever.

With a certain resolve, Mekari pulled out his cell phone.

2

After several rings, a female voice answered.

"Hello, this is the Kiyomaru Site."

"I would like to speak to Takaoki Ninagawa."

"This number is for answering questions. Please state your inquiry."

"My name is Mekari, and I'm an SP protecting Kiyomaru. Ask Mr. Ninagawa whether he has any interest in speaking with me."

"P-Please hold."

"I'll call back in five minutes."

He ended the call without waiting for her reply.

Kiyomaru stared at Mekari in shock.

"Wh-What the fuck are you doing?!"

"See, I thought I'd voice my complaints to old man Ninagawa…"

He didn't know himself what he was going to say. Was he telling Ninagawa to stop with this nonsense? He probably was. Not that it would actually change anything.

Kiyomaru didn't say more, and Mekari, too, waited silently.

Right when he tried to check his screen to see how many minutes it'd been, his cell started vibrating in his hand.

"This is Ninagawa."

Just as Mekari thought.

"Are you the one who's Kiyomaru's SP?"

"I'm Mekari, Security Section, Metropolitan Police."

"I was told that you sought an audience with me."

"You know, my partner and fellow SP died just a while ago. His head was blasted off with a shotgun…"

"…"

"To you, it might be no more than the death of a random police officer, but he had a name. Atsushi Shiraiwa. He had parents. Probably a lover as well. He hadn't even reached thirty…"

"…"

"He was stupid, but a really good guy…"

"…"

"Don't you have anything to say?"

"I think that's very unfortunate."

"Don't talk like it's got nothing to do with you! It's your fault, isn't it?!"

"Yes, it is my fault…"

"I've seen plenty of dead bodies and injured people today. Although I caused many of those injuries myself… Elsewhere too, lots of people have been mistaken for Kiyomaru and been murdered."

"So far, there have been eleven confirmed deaths."

"Are you okay with that?"

"…"

"Those people also had families. You're only increasing the number of people who'll share your suffering."

"That may be true…"

"Isn't this enough? Please just stop this foolishness."

"I also want to end this as soon as possible."

"Then—"

"However, there's only one way this can end. With Kiyomaru's death."

"You'd still go on about that?!"

"At the moment, you're the only one who knows where Kiyomaru is. You're the only one who can prevent any further, needless bloodshed…"

"Are you telling me to kill Kiyomaru?"

"Even if you kill Kiyomaru, you won't be held culpable. I guarantee it. Or is one billion not enough for you?"

"You're dead wrong if you think you can bribe everyone."

"Are you telling me you won't work for me?"

"That's right."

"You'll come to regret it."

"Don't worry about me."

"Why? Is it because you're a police officer? Is it your sense of responsibility as an SP?"

"No."

"Then your sense of justice as a person? Do you believe Kiyomaru is worth protecting with your life?"

"Of course not. Kiyomaru's nothing but human scum."

"Then why?"

"Because of you, Shiraiwa died."

"…"

"Why the hell should I work for you? Honestly, I want to kill you more than I do Kiyomaru."

"I see. Then we have nothing more to talk about…"

"Hey, wait!"

"What?"

"I think I understand where you're coming from. But you're doing this the wrong way."

"Every way is perfectly wrong."

"You think involving so many innocent people like this will make your granddaughter happy?!"

"I made a vow to my granddaughter. I can't change this."

"Remember your granddaughter's face! Imagine your grand-daughter's face as she's watching this conversation!"

Mekari always spoke to his dead wife. He felt certain that Ninagawa did the same.

Conversing with him now, he knew. Both of them were living tethered to the dead. They were the same breed.

"Doesn't she have tears in her eyes? Isn't she speaking to you with eyes brimming with tears? Try listening to her!"

"…"

"*Grandpa*—what does she say after that? *Grandpa*—listen closely to what she says after that! That's—"

The line went dead.

Kiyomaru was staring intently at Mekari.

"I guess the negotiations broke down," Mekari said with a wry smile.

Somehow his heart felt a little lighter. Was it because he'd said what he wanted to the ringleader of this mess?

The fix that Mekari was in had been starting to crush his soul. But now, all doubt had disappeared.

I can't lose to that old man, can I?

Suddenly—he felt hungry again.

"For now, I'll go get us some food. You can't even think on an empty stomach."

"Then I'll come too."

"No. I'm just going to that convenience store over there. You stay hidden here."

"But…"

"But what? I thought you trusted me."

"…"

"I'll be right back."

There was a taxi and several 50-cc scooters parked in the front lot of the convenience store.

Inside, there was an employee behind the cash register, and a woman of about thirty purchasing a can of coffee.

Five boys who looked around sixteen or seventeen stood in the magazines section; two more of around the same age, in the snacks corner. A fifty-something man was trying to pick out a boxed meal for himself.

No one paid attention to Mekari.

He tossed sandwiches and rice balls into his basket one after the other. Rounding to the refrigerators to purchase beverages, he added two small bottles of oolong tea. He walked around the store to see if there was anything he should buy other than food, but he couldn't think of anything.

One of the boys by the magazine rack jogged over to the two boys picking out chips.

"Listen. Don't look outside."

"What? Something outside the store?"

"Just promise not to look."

"Got it, I won't."

"So what's up?"

"There's this guy standing by himself out there who looks like, you know, Kiyomaru…"

"Seriously?!"

"Don't look. He'll run away."

Mekari put his basket down on the spot and headed towards the exit.

It was Kiyomaru sure enough.

Had he not been able to trust Mekari all the way? Or could he just not bear being alone? Either way, what a fool.

By the time Mekari got outside the store, four boys had already hemmed in his charge.

Mekari ran up to them. Three boys leapt out after him.

The two adults stood with their backs to the window of the store. Seven boys surrounded them.

"Holy shit, are you kidding me? It's really Kiyomaru."

"*Ka-ching*, one billion yen!"

Mekari took one step forward.

"Police, get out of the way."

But none of the boys were even listening to him.

"First, I'll stab him, and then we'll take turns making one stab at a time."

A bulky boy with a nose piercing who led the pack took out a folding knife from his pocket.

"Right, they won't be able to tell which stab killed him."

"Ah, so all of us get a billion each."

"Shit, we'll all be celebs."

The stupid-looking youths chattered excitedly amongst themselves.

Was it kids like them who killed homeless people for fun? Mekari was already tired of them.

"Move!"

He drew his SIG.

If Mekari were on his own, pulling a gun on such brats would have been unnecessary. He was positive he could suppress them with just his special baton.

But not while protecting Kiyomaru. No matter how much training you had as an SP, three was about the most you could handle at once. If Kiyomaru got stabbed by the others in the meantime, it'd be moot.

"Hey, hey, you can't really shoot, can you?" Nose Piercing was smirking. "We haven't done anything yet."

Mekari pointed the SIG at the kid's head and said, "Aren't you guys afraid of anything?"

"Nah," replied one of the brats.

"Oh, I've got one! The Great Tokai Earthquake."

All the brats burst into giggles.

"You've all seriously got some nerve." With his SIG still pointed at Nose Piercing, Mekari used his left hand to point at Kiyomaru behind him. "That guy's a serial killer, I've got a gun, and both of us are about to lose it."

The smirks slipped from the brats' faces. But they didn't make way.

Mekari knew all he had to do was shoot one of them in the knee. But it was true that the brats hadn't done anything yet.

Better if no one heard any gunfire.

"Stop trying to look cool, you can't shoot us," snorted Nose Piercing.

"Moment you fire, other six of us are rushing and stabbing you!" This came from a pimply brat on the far right who was brandishing a knife.

"We're minors, even we kill someone we get off easy," the bucktoothed kid to the left of Nose Piercing said, taking a step forward.

Every one of them had baby faces. They did their best to look grown-up, with their unshaven chins and flowing sideburns, but in the end they were just feeding off their parents and underestimating the world.

Mekari had seriously had enough.

After what I've been through, I have to listen to these brats talk rich?

If only Shiraiwa were there—Mekari would leave Kiyomaru to him and proceed to beat up the kids.

Kanbashi would have abandoned Kiyomaru and punched the kids bloody by now.

Would Sekiya calmly try to talk down even these brats?

No, if Kanbashi and Sekiya were there, the brats would have been too scared to pull this in the first place.

But no one was with him. Mekari was alone.

He was starting to not give a shit.

He stretched out his right arm holding the SIG. He slowly raised it to eye level.

The brats all gulped.

"If you shoot us *you* get the death sentence!" barked Nose Piercing.

Mekari matched the white dot in the front sight of the SIG with the valley of the viewfinder and aimed for Nose Piercing's forehead.

He wanted to see the other brats' faces after he shot Nose Piercing in the head.

He wanted, so badly, to see exactly how much Nose Piercing's close-shaven noggin would swell and warp if a 9 mm Silver-tip punching into his forehead hollowed out his cranium instead of piercing through.

He remembered the manga *Fist of the North Star*, popular in the old days. He recalled the shapes the villains' heads took when their secret pressure spots were struck by Kenshiro.

The bad guys yelped, *Hi-de-bu.*

A laugh spilled out from Mekari's lips.

"Ahhhhh—!!"

Nose Piercing jumped back as though he had just touched a high-voltage wire.

As one, the other brats also fled toward the road.

Mekari couldn't readily tell what had happened. The kids all vanished in a split second.

A woman was watching.

Standing by the store's entrance and sipping her coffee, the woman who'd been inside was watching.

"Shouldn't you get out of here quick?"

She was right.

The brats might put in a call to the police to try to get even.

No, the store employee may have already tipped them off.

But returning to the unmanned police box was too dangerous now. The brats might still be watching.

Mekari was out of places to go. Where could they possibly run?

"Want a lift?"

The woman pointed at the cab parked in front of them.

3

He couldn't tell what the woman's intentions were. Why had she offered them a helping hand?

Mekari and Kiyomaru sat in the back of the cab.

The ID card in front of the passenger's seat had a photo of the woman's face and gave her name in Chinese characters. Mekari supposed you read it "Chikako Yuri."

Not a local cabbie for nothing, she steered through alleys that were impressively clear of any police presence. But it was dangerous to keep driving.

They'd already come quite a ways from the convenience store. Mekari made her stop in an empty street.

"Why did you help us?" he asked her.

"Help? I'm going to charge you, you know."

"No, of course we'll pay, I meant—"

"Well, it's a taxi driver's job to drive around passengers…"

"Aren't you interested in the billion?"

"Ha ha ha… If I thought I could kill him."

It was bizarre how relaxed she was.

"See, the news has been going on and on about how Kiyomaru stole a gun and took an officer hostage and is on the run. But just a moment ago, I witnessed with my own eyes that that's not true. How interesting, right?"

"…"

"Well, if it were just Kiyomaru, I wouldn't have let him on, but there's a reliable-looking detective with him…"

Mekari was about to say, "I'm not a detective," but thought better of it. The difference wouldn't mean anything to her.

"Since we're doing this anyway, I'd appreciate a *long* ride…" she invited using the English word—cabbie argot.

"Um, if it were possible, I'd of course like to be taken to Kasumigaseki in Tokyo, but…"

"Wow! The first out-of-prefecture fare in a while. Business's been pretty bad lately, you know."

It seemed like Yuri was in a fine mood. Or maybe she was always like this.

Mekari felt disoriented. She wasn't on the same wavelength as the situation he and Kiyomaru were in.

"Forget it," Mekari said. "We won't make it past the checkpoint."

"The inspections today are intense! There's police everywhere. Oops, looks like here too, ha ha ha…"

The woman laughed a lot. When she did, her eyes turned into slits.

Mekari tried to explain to Yuri. If the police found them, Kiyomaru would be shot on sight.

"Huh, how awful. Can't trust the police."

"…"

"I think we'll manage though," Yuri assured casually.

The taxi drove through the city of Iwata and into Kakegawa. Yuri spotted a convenience store in an alley and parked a short distance away.

"I'll go buy some food for you guys," she said, thrusting her hand in front of Mekari.

When he placed a ten-thousand-yen bill there, she got out of the driver's seat and ran off to the store.

Could they really get past the checkpoint by following Yuri's plan? Quite possibly, but it wasn't sure-fire.

"That woman isn't gonna report us, I hope?" Kiyomaru said, sounding fairly anxious.

"If that was her plan, she wouldn't have let us on in the first place."

"Then maybe she's calling her husband and telling him to bring the kitchen knife…"

"Hey, do you really think that?"

"No…"

Kiyomaru didn't say anything else.

Mekari wasn't feeling inclined to doubt Yuri one bit.

He wondered why. She'd lifted them out of a cul-de-sac, sure. Those friendly facial expressions, sure.

She came back with a bulging convenience store bag hanging from her arm.

Handing it, the change, and the receipt to Mekari, Yuri said,

215

"If you can't eat it all, I'll take responsibility and help out."

The bag contained two boxed meals and a ton of sandwiches and rice balls. The drinks comprised tea, milk, cola, a cafe latte, and milk tea with tapioca.

She'd clearly bought some of it for herself.

"There's no way we can finish this all. We need your help," Mekari said, offering Yuri the milk tea with tapioca.

"Was it that obvious? Ha ha ha…"

Yuri wasn't a complicated one.

Kiyomaru started devouring the chicken cutlet set at a furious pace. Mekari stuffed a rice ball in his mouth.

The tuna mayonnaise flavor tasted absurdly delicious.

True, he hadn't had a meal for almost seventeen hours since breakfast.

Even so, it seemed odd considering their predicament.

The awful day had yet to come to an end. Their lives were still in danger.

Yuri was gobbling up a sandwich, too.

Mekari reached out to grab a second rice ball. This time it was roasted cod roe flavor.

No one said a word as they ate.

Mekari was enjoying having something delicious. He couldn't believe it.

He hadn't felt that way since his wife had died.

Yuri said that she'd already been inspected four times that day. According to her, the officers conducting the checks were pretty indifferent towards taxis. Not once had they asked to see her driver's license, and they hadn't opened her trunk.

They simply peered into her back seat, and when her fare was elderly or a young couple, she was let through immediately. The two times she didn't have customers, they didn't even order her to stop.

"Are you still worried? We'll definitely be fine."

It was bizarre that at Yuri's words, Mekari felt as though it really would be fine.

Kiyomaru lay on his side in the trunk. He looked stressed. "Actually, let's not do this," he said. "I'm claustrophobic…"

"Can't have everything," Mekari scolded and slammed the trunk closed.

He undid the magazine pouch and the special baton from his waist and placed both in his jacket. The one remaining spare magazine he stuck in his pants pocket. He tossed the jacket on the passenger's seat and got in the driver's side in just his buttoned shirt and tie.

As a precaution, he drew his SIG and hid it beneath his thigh.

Yuri was lounging in the back seat.

"Whoo, this is great. Feels so luxurious."

She'd dropped her green uniform jacket to the floor.

No matter how you looked at it, they were a taxi with one female passenger. Yuri insisted that with this setup they'd surely pass any inspection.

Mekari decided to risk it. It wasn't like they had any other option.

But it would be all over if they asked Mekari, the fake driver, to show his ID. Even if the local police didn't recognize his face, they'd certainly perk up at his name.

Maybe they didn't check Yuri's ID because she was a female driver.

Just in case, Mekari decided to take an extra precaution.

4

Guided by Yuri, Mekari raced the taxi down back alleys. He wasn't used to the gear stick, which made it difficult to drive. The area around the Tokyo-Nagoya or Tomei Expressway's Kakegawa IC was congested due to the inspections.

Mekari took out his cell phone.

"What's close to the Kakegawa Interchange entrance?"

"Hmm, let's see, the municipal general hospital's right nearby. What else is there…"

Without waiting for Yuri to continue, Mekari dialed 110, the emergency police number.

"This is Mekari of the Metropolitan Police Security Section. Kiyomaru doesn't know that I'm making this call. Please look up this cell phone number to confirm. He's currently hiding on the premises of the Kakegawa Municipal General Hospital. Requesting that you search here immediately."

Mekari did all the talking and ended the call.

"Whoa, that was so cool…" cheered Yuri, as happy-go-lucky as ever.

The Kakegawa IC entrance checkpoint was going to be turned upside down. They'd need to send personnel over to the hospital. Unless a vehicle was exceedingly suspicious, they might not even inspect it properly.

The checkpoint was slowly approaching. A large number of police cruisers were parked on the shoulder of the road, and many officers were moving around. It looked like Mekari's call hadn't taken effect yet.

It was almost their turn.

The car in front of them was having its trunk opened. Mekari's heart leapt into his throat.

A young uniformed officer walked up to the taxi. "Sorry about this," he said, peering in.

"You haven't found Kiyomaru yet?" Yuri asked, dragging on her cigarette.

The greenhorn still had some adolescence left in his features, but he was plenty terrifying.

Mekari prayed that he wasn't looking too tense.

He suddenly realized that the driver ID by the passenger seat was still there. If it… His armpits began to sweat.

Suddenly, the newbie officer pressed his finger to the microphone in his ear and turned aside.

He waved his hand, urging them forward. Mekari took his time on purpose.

The taxi passed inspection and entered the Tomei Expressway from Kakegawa IC.

Mekari's heart still wouldn't settle. Yuri was cackling on the back seat.

They continued for a while after passing the tollgate and parked at a recess. Mekari waited for a break in the vehicles overtaking them and quickly let Kiyomaru out from the trunk.

Kiyomaru didn't seem to know yet that they were past the checkpoint.

Yuri moved back to the driver's seat. Mekari got in the back with Kiyomaru.

"Hey, don't forget this." Yuri handed Mekari his SIG.

"Thank you. We owe you our lives."

"Ha ha ha… But it's still too early to celebrate. First, let's get out of Shizuoka."

She was absolutely right. She tended to be.

Yuri returned the taxi to the cruising lane and made good time.

"Hey, we're leaving Shizuoka soon."

When Mekari came to, the taxi was stopped. He had somehow fallen asleep.

"Where are we?"

"The Ashigara Service Area."

They'd come all the way to Gotenba while he slept. Kanagawa, the prefecture just south of Tokyo, was only a hop away.

There was a good chance there'd be another checkpoint at the prefectural border. They put Kiyomaru in the trunk once again. Mekari drove the taxi out of Ashigara SA and cleared the Takao and Sakuradaira tunnels.

The border was coming up.

Ahead, the Kanagawa Police were conducting inspections. Mekari slowed down as he approached the checkpoint.

The uniformed officer gestured a "Go" with a sweep of his

flag. Mekari passed through.

The station wagon directly behind them was ordered to stop. Mekari stepped on the accelerator.

The checkpoint shrank in the mirror.

It had been so easy. Mekari was almost disappointed.

They drove into Ayuzawa PA and stopped. Mekari unlocked the trunk and got out from the driver's seat. Yuri also got off and stood next to him at the car's rear.

Kiyomaru shoved open the trunk and stuck his head out.

"Where are we?"

"In Kanagawa."

At Mekari's words, Kiyomaru's face crinkled.

Seeing him smile, Yuri laughed. Mekari's lips relaxed too, in spite of himself.

They'd finally managed to escape Shizuoka prefecture. Right now, no one knew where they were. The police probably didn't doubt that they were still hiding out in Shizuoka.

All they needed to do now was keep driving down the Tomei Expressway. In around two hours, they'd reach the Metropolitan Police Department.

It was all thanks to Yuri. Mekari believed that from the bottom of his heart.

His eyes met with hers. He hastily looked away.

Realizing that he was finding Yuri attractive, Mekari felt guilty.

With Yuri driving once again, they were making good progress through Kanagawa.

The car radio was playing a commercial station's late night program. It took Mekari back to his student days.

They were almost in Tokyo. Soon, very soon, he'd be freed of this miserable job.

When this was all over, he wondered if he could offer to take Yuri out to dinner to express his thanks.

Would she turn him down?

No, he only meant to show his appreciation, he didn't mean anything else by it.

Mekari was making excuses to himself.

The radio switched to a news program.

He was about to hear them report that Kiyomaru was still hiding in Shizuoka and hadn't been found. He almost felt giddy.

But instead of Shizuoka, the female host spoke of Hokkaido.

"Last night at around 11 p.m. in Kushiro, Hokkaido, suspect Kunihide Kiyomaru's mother was found dead, having hanged herself."

The air in the cab seemed to freeze.

"After inspecting the scene, and given the will left on the kitchen table, police believe that suicide is the most likely—"

Mekari looked at Kiyomaru. His eyes were opened so wide they looked like they would tear at the corners.

"The will reads, 'My dear Kuni, I beg you upon my life. Please don't do anything bad anymore. Please don't hurt other people anymore. I beg you. I'll go on ahead and wait for you. Don't always be leaving your mother alone by herself. To Kunihide Kiyomaru'—"

Kiyomaru's body was trembling. A sob leaked from his

mouth. He covered his face with both his manacled hands and wept.

Mekari's moment of joy had vanished. He noticed that Yuri was crying, too. Her steering was unstable.

She decelerated and parked at a recess. She kept on crying, silently.

"Let's switch," he called to Yuri and got out of the car. She sniffled and moved over to the passenger's seat.

Mekari sat behind the wheel and started driving.

At this late time of night, almost all of the cars were going at a considerable speed. Mekari entered the fast lane.

He matched the flow and raced onwards. When he checked the meter, they were going at 120 km.

Yuri turned around and gently placed a hand on Kiyomaru's shoulder.

"Please, live to your fullest for your mother…"

Kiyomaru's sobs grew louder.

Yuri turned back to the front and wiped her tears on her sleeve.

The radio station had proceeded to a music program in the meantime. A nostalgic pop song was playing.

"Tokyo 1 km," a sign said. Soon, very soon…

But now Mekari only felt bitter.

Whether or not he was feeling sympathy for Kiyomaru, he didn't know.

But he certainly felt bad for Kiyomaru's mother. She'd died believing that Kiyomaru had taken him hostage and was on the run.

All of a sudden, Kiyomaru sat up, leaned towards the passenger's seat, and wrapped his arms around Yuri's throat.

A groan spilled from her mouth. Mekari took his left hand off the wheel and struck Kiyomaru. But nearly crashing into a car on the cruising lane, he quickly faced forward again.

Yuri was struggling, kicking both her feet. If he stepped on the break, the car right behind would ram into them.

Mekari feared for his own sanity.

5

He cut the wheel to the right.

The car's body screeched against the side of the highway divider. The fender mirror broke off.

The entire car shook. But Kiyomaru didn't let go of Yuri's neck.

Mekari stepped on the accelerator again. A fearsome spray of sparks erupted from the car's flank.

All around, other vehicles maintained a fraught distance. Mekari forcefully cut into the slow lane.

This time he veered the wheel to the left and crashed the body of the car against the left wall. The remaining fender mirror broke off in another spray of sparks.

The car ahead of them fled to the fast lane. Mekari kept his foot on the accelerator.

A recess was approaching on the left. Without slowing down, Mekari cut the wheel to the left. He crashed the car's flank into the wall to come to a halt.

The impact was quite something.

Kiyomaru didn't let go of Yuri even then. She had stopped kicking her legs.

Mekari punched Kiyomaru in the face. The guy still didn't let go. A second time. A third. A fourth. Kiyomaru finally relented.

Yuri's neck was bent in an unnatural direction. Her eyes were wide open but she didn't budge.

Her neck had snapped.

Mekari immediately checked for her vital signs.

He put his palm and ear close to her nose and mouth. She wasn't breathing.

He touched the inside of her wrist. He couldn't feel her pulse.

He pressed his ear to her chest to try to hear her heart itself. There was no beat.

Her heart had stopped.

Usually, if a person wasn't breathing and had no pulse, after securing the airway you attempted CPR. That much, an SP like Mekari had been trained in.

But how did you secure the airway of someone whose neck had snapped? He couldn't even touch her neck.

"Heh, bitch was getting too full of herself!" spat Kiyomaru.

It made no sense.

In the end, Kiyomaru wasn't a creature Mekari could understand.

He punched Kiyomaru; his nose broke and blood burst out.

Another punch. Blood spewed from Kiyomaru's mouth. And another punch. Punch. Punch punch punch punch punch—

Mekari felt a sharp pain. One of Kiyomaru's broken teeth had stuck into his right fist.

The guy's face was completely bloodied. His left eyelid had swollen up, sealing his eye.

"Do you want to kill me?" piped Kiyomaru, blood dribbling from his lips. "I bet you do. Come on, kill me."

Mekari drew his SIG. He pointed it at Kiyomaru's head.

"I'm going to get killed anyway. Once we reach the Metropolitan Police, you might be all done, but people will keep coming after me until I'm dead."

So what. Who cares.

"But I haven't done enough to deserve the death sentence. If I'm going to be killed anyway, I might as well commit the crimes."

What the hell had Mekari been doing until now?

Okumura had said it. Ninagawa had said it.

There would come a time when he'd regret letting Kiyomaru live.

That time was now.

Yuri would die. No, maybe she was already dead. He couldn't tell.

Mekari couldn't do anything for her. He couldn't save her. Even though she'd saved him.

This is my fault.

At this point, he just needed to kill Kiyomaru.

In that case, he ought to have done it sooner.

If he had, Yuri wouldn't have had to die.

Shiraiwa wouldn't have had to die, either.

Maybe even Kiyomaru's mother, too.

I kill Kiyomaru, and then what?

There was nothing left but to die. He'd die and rejoin his wife.

Mekari aimed for Kiyomaru's right eye.

It was looking straight at Mekari. There was no fear in Kiyomaru's expression.

There was even a faint smile on his lips.

Mekari's right index finger slowly squeezed the trigger.

That was when the music station cut to the voice of an announcer.

"We apologize for the interruption to your music, but we have some news. The bounty placed on suspect Kunihide Kiyomaru by Mr. Takaoki Ninagawa has been revoked."

Mekari thought he'd misheard.

Kiyomaru looked dumbfounded.

"Mr. Ninagawa himself just sent a message to various media outlets by fax. The reason for the revocation is unclear, but we presume it was a decision made in response to the suspect's mother's suicide."

Apparently the Kiyomaru Site's content had been revised entirely, and it was now beaming the revocation of the bounty.

The news added that in sync with Ninagawa's change of mind, the National Police Agency had revoked its orders to shoot Kiyomaru on sight.

Kiyomaru looked unsettled. He seemed unable to decide how to deal with this turn of events. Not a trace of his burst of cockiness remained on his uncertain mug.

Mekari felt all the strength seep out of himself. He lowered the SIG and sank down into the seat.

He pulled out his cell phone and called Subsection Chief Ohki.

Then, he lit his second cigarette of the day.

An ambulance arrived before Mekari could turn one Seven Star into a pile of ash. A squad of police cars also came.

Yuri was placed on the ambulance and taken away. But it didn't seem like she could be resuscitated, not by a long shot.

Mekari and Kiyomaru sat side by side in the back of a cruiser. Neither of them said a word.

Sandwiched on the front and rear by PCs, they traveled along Metropolitan Expressway 3.

The bounty on Kiyomaru had been revoked. No one should be coming after him now.

Mekari wondered if his attempt to persuade Ninagawa had had any effect.

But it was too late.

Had Ninagawa made his decision just a little sooner, Yuri might still be breathing.

Was Kiyomaru going to be sentenced to death now?

Hunted by the whole country and with nowhere to turn, there was no question that Kiyomaru had been in an abnormal state of mind.

Mekari had no idea how the judge would assess that.

The night was almost over.

They exited the expressway on the Kasumigaseki Ramp. Sakuradamon, where the MPD was located, was close by.

They turned right just past the Ministry of Foreign Affairs, then left at the first block. They rounded Joint Bureau Building No. 2, which housed the Metropolitan Police.

Press were overflowing in front of the MPD HQ building.

When they noticed the column of police cars with Mekari and began to rush close, a 4WD parked on a curb suddenly shot forward and crashed into the lead vehicle.

The driver of the cruiser that Mekari and Kiyomaru were on hit the brakes, but they collided into the stalled lead vehicle.

The impact was tremendous. Then the car behind them rammed into their rear.

Mekari floated, then fell just as soon.

Pain shot through his entire body.

He glanced around even as his consciousness flickered.

Kiyomaru's head had gone through the door window. Glass shards littered his body and he was passed out.

The officers in the driver and passenger seats were wiggling, pinned by their airbags.

A man leapt out of the 4WD that had bull rushed the lead police car.

He approached the one Mekari and Kiyomaru were in. The door on Mekari's side opened.

The man looked around forty. He gripped a kitchen knife in his right hand.

By the time Mekari pulled out his SIG, Kiyomaru had already been stabbed.

Fresh blood spewed from the nape of his neck.

Covering Kiyomaru's body with his own, Mekari pointed his

gun at the man.

"Haven't you heard?! You won't get a billion anymore for killing this guy!"

Tears streamed from the man's eyes.

"I'm the father of Megumi, whom he murdered seven years ago."

"!"

"Please, let me kill Kiyomaru."

So there was one man in the world who hadn't come to kill Kiyomaru for the money.

Returning to society after only seven years when he'd slaughtered the man's daughter was unforgivable enough, but Kiyomaru had killed another girl soon after being released. He hadn't repented one bit.

Mekari could understand this father's feelings.

The man had the right to kill Kiyomaru.

If anyone was going to, Mekari wanted it to be this man.

"I have no intention of hurting you. Please, get out of my way."

The man's voice was calm.

His face was resolve itself.

Mekari lowered his SIG. He couldn't shoot this man.

"Stop!" shouted the officer in the driver's seat. He'd undone his seatbelt and turned around.

The uniformed cops in the cars to the front and rear finally came crawling out.

"Drop your weapon!"

They surrounded the man and pointed their guns at him. The man ignored them and tried to pounce on Kiyomaru.

One of the officers fired. The report filled the dawn air outside the Imperial Palace.

The man fell to the ground, shot through the thigh. Cops swarmed over him in an instant, hiding him from sight.

The press came running and camera shutters clicked everywhere.

They were getting shots of Mekari and Kiyomaru too. Mekari was blinded for a moment by the successive flashes.

He slowly sat up. His whole body ached, but it wasn't so bad that he couldn't move.

His mind was finally clearing. He holstered the SIG and pulled Kiyomaru straight.

Blood bubbled out of the wounds to Kiyomaru's mouth and neck. It was proof that he was breathing.

Propping Kiyomaru up, Mekari stepped out of the car.

The press had them surrounded by now.

The strobe lights of the cameras flashed ceaselessly. Multiple ENG Cameras for television were also trained on them.

Mekari walked towards the MPD HQ building.

Uniformed police came rushing and made the press step back. An absurd number of media personnel moved along with Mekari as he lugged Kiyomaru.

Mekari climbed the stone steps in front of HQ's main entrance, one step at a time.

He had finally managed to get here.

He'd brought Kiyomaru here alive.

He'd carried out the mission he'd been tasked with.

Yet, he felt no sense of accomplishment whatsoever.

Is Kiyomaru going to live on?

Did my actions mean anything?

How does my wife see me now?

Kiyomaru moved his lips as though he wanted to say something. All that came out was a bloody froth.

What had he meant to say?

But none of it mattered anymore.

Damn it all!

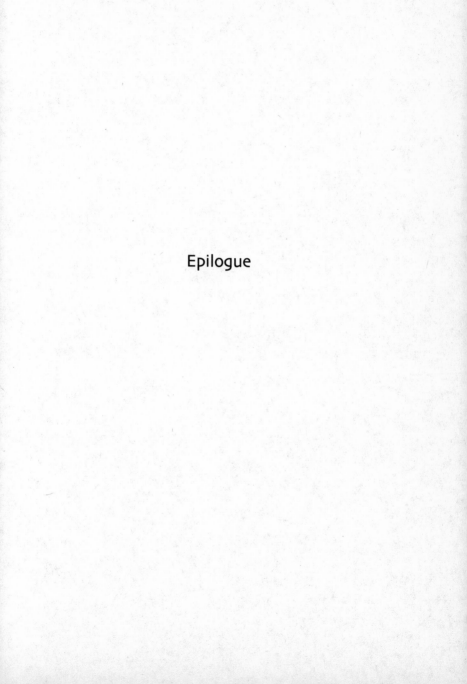

Epilogue

"Are you satisfied?" Saraya asked.

Ninagawa didn't answer.

He was gazing at the TV screen.

The man who entered the Metropolitan Police Headquarters just now, hauling Kiyomaru.

So that was Mekari.

What a severe-looking fellow.

Yet he'd also looked as though he were wrapped in grief.

Several streams of blood had been running down his face. Even so, his footsteps had been firm.

So that's the man I lost to.

Ninagawa was tasting defeat. Of course he wasn't satisfied.

Yet he couldn't voice his feelings.

The reason why he hadn't obtained satisfying results was that his will had cracked. Ever since his phone conversation with Mekari, Chika's voice had called to him in his head.

He couldn't go against that voice.

"I knew you'd do that," Saraya said—as always, as though he saw through everything. "Myself, I'm satisfied. I've been compensated sufficiently, and nothing beyond my expectations occurred…"

Well then, he said and turned his back to Ninagawa.

Kazuhiro Kiuchi

The devil in the tired suit left the hospital chamber, not so much as glancing over his shoulder.

ABOUT THE AUTHOR

Legendary manga milestone *Be-Bop High School* creator Kazuhiro Kiuchi made his debut as a novelist in 2004 with *Shield of Straw*. Another of his growing list of prose offerings, *A Dog in Water*, is also available in English.

ALSO BY THE SAME AUTHOR

A Dog in Water

ISBN 978-1-939130-03-7
Trade Paperback, $14.95/16.95

Selected as one of *The Strand Magazine*'s Top 20 Books of 2013

Until pain, memory, resignation and fury all alike are subsumed by the one possible conclusion, a thing or two may just be worth doing. Thus a nameless former cop who should never have become a private detective awaits clients in a dingy office across the street from a Chinese restaurant. Impeccably paced and snappily told even when the truth grows murky, hardboiled has never come as smooth or as pure as in this choice distillation by way of Tokyo. Warning: no dogs cute or otherwise appear in this work, in or out of water.

"Between the semi-serialized storytelling and the rich detail the author presents, *A Dog in Water* is a unique take on what constitutes a detective novel. The ending builds over each case, each gunshot, and each body shot, culminating in an unexpected ending that feels earned as the lines between black and white turn a thick, hazy gray."
—*Bookslut*

MORE MYSTERY FROM VERTICAL

Pro Bono
by Seicho Matsumoto
ISBN 978-1-934287-02-6, $14.95/16.95

From the father of postwar Japanese mystery who steered the genre away from locked rooms and toward a wider world of social forces, a classic about a young woman's revenge against a renowned lawyer.

City of Refuge
by Kenzo Kitakata
ISBN 978-1-934287-12-5, $14.95/18.95

It was only when the don of Japanese hardboiled came onto the scene in the '80s that the style truly became homegrown, weaning itself of anti-heroes with native names and foreign mannerisms.

Naoko
by Keigo Higashino
ISBN 978-1-932234-07-7, $14.95/19.95

Winner of the Japan Mystery Writers Award, this black comedy of hidden minds and lives turned the author, one of Japan's most ambitious and versatile mystery hands, into a perennial favorite.

KIZUMONOGATARI: Wound Tale
by NISIOISIN
ISBN 978-1-941220-97-9, $14.95/17.95

It doesn't get more cutting edge than this genre-traversing work by the palindromic mystery writer, the leading light of a younger generation who began their careers in the twenty-first century.

Learn more at www.vertical-inc.com